GONE

BALLISTIC

A Robin Starling Legal Thriller
Volume 6

GONE
BALLISTIC

Michael Monhollon

Reflection Publishing
Abilene, Texas

For Rachel, always

Chapter 1

The short-barreled pistol slid from the Priority Mail box amid a jumble of styrofoam peanuts. It landed with a clunk on my desk, where it lay bristling with switches and sights, its matte black finish absorbing light. "Whoa," Brooke said, stopping in the doorway of my office. "You got yourself a gun."

I looked up. "I didn't. It came in the mail."

"Somebody sent you a gun? Who?"

I looked at the flat-rate box the gun had come in. My address was hand-printed in block letters. There was no return address. "No idea." I looked inside the box, then shook out the remaining peanuts. No packing list. The styrofoam peanuts were all there were.

"Why?" Brooke asked.

"If I knew who, I might know why."

"I'll bet Paul ordered it for you for protection. He's worried about you ever since…you know."

Ever since I'd been shot in the head. I did know.

"This doesn't seem like Paul," I said. "And why wouldn't there be a packing list?"

1

Paul Soldano—my boyfriend, for lack of a better word—had an unusual knack for showing up whenever we talked about him, but this time my doorway remained empty. He did have a job, after all, and as a bank examiner for the Federal Reserve Bank of Richmond, he was often not even in town.

I picked up my trashcan and used the empty box to sweep the styrofoam peanuts from around the gun and off my desk. The pistol lay by itself on the polished surface. Brooke leaned over it.

"What?" I said.

"It smells like firecrackers."

I leaned over it and took a sniff. "Okay," I said.

"I think that means it's been fired."

"I didn't know you knew guns."

"I don't really. Well, I know this one's a semiautomatic and not a revolver, but that's about it. On TV, though, people are always sniffing gun barrels to see if they've been fired."

"Ah."

"I wonder if Rodney's in his office. I'll go check." The executive suites where we had our offices took up an entire floor, but Rodney Burns was close. He had the third office in our cluster of three. A private detective who looked a little like Don Knotts with a caterpillar stapled to his upper lip, Rodney had always done good work for me. When he came back with Brooke, he was pulling on a pair of latex gloves.

"So that's the gun," he said.

"I was hoping for a little more in the way of expert analysis," I said.

He sniffed it. "What do you want me to do with it?"

"Has it been fired?"

"At some point. You don't know who sent it?"

I held up the box. "No return address. No packing slip. Just the gun and a bunch of plastic peanuts."

He picked up the gun, gingerly, despite his latex gloves, and ejected the magazine.

"Is there an exploded cartridge in there?" Brooke asked.

Rodney smiled at her. "There's room for another bullet," he said, pressing down on them, "so one might have been fired since it was loaded. This isn't a revolver, though. It ejects the empty casings as the bullets fire."

"Oh." So Brooke really didn't know more about guns than I did—maybe even less. I had been forced to read up on them since I'd started representing murder defendants, though my knowledge was largely academic.

"Why would someone send it to me?"

They both looked at me.

"Right," I said. "How would you know?"

"Let me get the serial number," Rodney said. "I can find out who the last registered purchaser was."

The elevator doors were sliding shut as Brooke and I pushed through the glass doors of the Executive Suites, but they bounced open again without quite closing. One of the newer tenants smiled at us as we got on with him. He was a small man who looked like Rock Hudson might have looked if he'd been five-six and had oily hair and a big hooked nose—which I suppose is another way of saying he didn't look like Rock Hudson at all.

"Thanks," I said.

"Thank you. It's not every day I get to share an elevator with two such beautiful women."

The expression I gave him was about halfway between a grimace and a smile.

"Carter Fox," he said, holding out a hand.

"You're the new lawyer who just moved in, aren't you?" I said as I shook his hand. "There are three of us now."

"Then you're Robin Starling. At least, you don't look like you could be Dave Johnstone."

"No. Not very easily." I retrieved my hand with a small jerk.

"Not without extensive surgery, anyway." Carter gave a honk of laughter. "Sorry. Not funny. Are you ladies going to lunch?" The elevator doors opened on the ground floor.

Brooke gave me a hard look over his shoulder as we got out.

"We're meeting someone," I said.

"The reason I asked, I'm new to downtown, and I need to find a good place to take on fuel for the battles of the afternoon."

"The restaurant in the basement of this building's not half-bad."

"If you don't mind, I'll just tag along with you ladies, see where the natives eat, you know. Don't worry about me horning in on your lunch party. I wouldn't do that. Besides, I brought along my favorite dining companion." He held up a mini-tablet with a pebbled black cover, possibly a Kindle.

He walked between us as we went down Main Street toward Twelfth. The sky was blue, and the sun was beginning to cut through the morning chill.

"It looks like it's going to be a good day," I said. "We could have left our jackets."

"A redhead and a blonde," Carter said, not to be distracted by talk of the weather. "If my old fraternity brothers could see me now."

I was the blonde in the mix. Goose bumps broke out on my arm closest to him as the skin tried to crawl away.

There was a line at our usual burger place almost to the door.

"This is it, huh?" Carter said as he stepped forward to pull open the door for us. "The favorite eating spot."

"Well, today," I said.

"I'm looking forward to it. When the top woman lawyer in the city of Richmond likes a place, I'm willing to give it a try."

On the other side of him, Brooke rolled her eyes. There were maybe a dozen people in front of us, but usually the line moved pretty fast.

Carter turned to Brooke. "What do you do for a living? I mean, beyond gladdening the hearts of men everywhere?"

For a moment I thought she wouldn't answer, but she said, "I'm an I.T. person. Mostly I help small and medium-sized businesses put together their computer systems."

"Wow," he said. I thought he would let it go at that, but he added, "Beautiful and smart. I have to tell you, that dark red hair is really special, and your clothes make the most of it. You have excellent taste."

By the time we got to the counter, he had us as well-oiled as a couple of limp French fries. I ordered a hamburger with mustard and all the vegetables. Brooke, more virtuous than I, got a grilled chicken sandwich. As Carter stepped up to order, Brooke led us decisively to a table in the corner with no empty tables around it. When Carter turned with his own tray, he was left with the choice of a couple of empty tables on the other side of the restaurant.

"He's going to see we weren't really meeting anyone," I said as he headed away from us.

"So?"

"Unless Mike is getting back from Farmville."

She shook her head. "His hearing was at ten. Or maybe ten-thirty. I wasn't really listening."

"It's only an hour drive, an hour fifteen minutes. He could be back any time."

Neither of us did a very good job of keeping up with our men. Mike had actually asked Brooke to marry him, but so far she'd avoided giving him an answer. Technically, I guess, she had agreed to marry him, but had avoided setting a date. Returning to our mistreatment of the oily Mr. Fox, I said, "He's a new guy with no one to hang out with, and we're just as cliquish as they come."

"You can't make me feel bad about it." She bit violently into her sandwich. "I feel like I need a shower."

"Oh, come on. He likes you. He likes your hair, your taste in clothes, probably your neat little figure and everything else about you."

She swallowed. "It makes me sick. Surely you're not falling for all glib flattery, Miss Top-Woman-Lawyer-in-the-city-of-Richmond."

"You thought that was insincere? I just took it as my due." I bit into my hamburger and chewed reflectively. When I'd swallowed, I said, "The woman-lawyer qualification always gripes me, though. It's like I don't compete in the same category as men, as if trial work were like track or basketball." In college I'd played basketball on a team that made it to the Final Four—Division Three, but still. Even so, our team wouldn't have beat the men's, despite its losing season.

"See? You don't like him either," Brooke said.

"I never said I liked him. I was just wondering how it would feel to be a more charitable person."

When we'd finished eating, Carter Fox was only halfway through his hamburger, reading his Kindle or his iPad mini or whatever it was and glancing at us from time to time. I took a breath and stood up. "I'm going to buy him an ice cream cone."

"Robin!"

"Don't argue. I feel myself in danger of becoming the kind of woman I despise."

Carter looked up as we approached, then nearly knocked over his chair getting to his feet.

"We got stood up," I said. "Here. We bought you desert."

"Well, thank you. Thank you very much." He took the ice cream cone and stood it on its base beside his tray. "I look forward to eating it." He seemed uncertain as to whether to sit or to remain standing, so I put him out of his misery by pulling out a chair and sitting in it. Brooke sat, too, and to her credit refrained from scowling.

"If you don't mind my asking, who would stand up two such beautiful women as yourselves?"

"My boyfriend's out of town. Brooke's fiancé was supposed to be here, but evidently he's still on his way back from Farmville."

"Who's the lucky man?" Carter asked her, and Brooke looked at me inquiringly.

"Lawyer named Mike McMillan," I said.

"He practice here in Richmond?"

"He does. Has his own practice."

"So when's the big date?"

I looked at Brooke, who now looked annoyed.

"We haven't set it," she said. "We..." She broke off, shrugged.

"Every man needs a wife, especially a lawyer," Carter said, sounding wistful. "When you go out into the world, you need someone tending the home fires, someone to be there when they carry you home on your shield."

"I never thought of it that way," Brooke said, standing. "I guess if I'm going to be there to tend the home fires for Mike this evening, I'd better get some work done."

"Especially since no one's with him to carry him home on his shield," I said, standing too.

Carter picked up his ice cream cone. "I'll walk back with you," he said, picking up his tray with his other hand. "If I'd realized how big the burger was, I wouldn't have gotten fries."

"Well, that was a bust," Brooke said when we were back in our office cluster and Carter Fox had gone back to his lair deeper in the labyrinth of the Executive Suites. "Mr. Oily walks us to and from lunch, and all the time we're not having to talk to him, you're feeling guilty about not talking to him."

"That last reference to my long legs went a long way toward curing me," I said, reaching into my purse for my keys.

"Don't forget your athletic physique."

"Don't remind me." Carter had also wanted to know about my lucky man, which I somehow found more intrusive than his questions about Brooke's. I looked down into my purse, which I held open with both hands. I had a wallet in there, my cell phone, a comb, a pen, some ChapStick, a PocketPak of Listerine breath strips...but no keys.

Rodney came out of his office. "Have a good lunch?" he said.

I opened my mouth to tell him not to ask, saw Brooke with her mouth open, evidently to tell him the same thing, and burst out laughing. She closed her mouth, smiled, and started laughing, too. Rodney looked back and forth between us.

"What?" he said. "Did I say something funny?"

He hadn't, of course. What he had done was get a name, address, and phone number for the purchaser of the Smith & Wesson semiautomatic that was in my desk drawer.

"I left my keys on my desk," I said. "Let me get Carly to let me in, and I'll come see what you have."

I went to find Carly, and Brooke went down the hall to off-load the tea she'd had with lunch.

"I always put my keys in my purse," Carly said virtuously. "That way I don't forget them."

I sometimes did that. Other times I dropped them on my desk or the credenza behind it...or sometimes on a bookshelf.

"This is only the second time you've had to unlock the door for me," I said.

She raised her eyebrows.

"Or third," I amended.

She pushed my door open and stepped back. "It's okay. All part of the service," she said.

I intended to put my keys in my purse immediately, but I didn't see them. I opened the drawer to put my purse away, saw the automatic, and closed it again. I left my purse on the floor in the desk's kneehole and headed for Rodney's office, glancing into Brooke's on the way to see if I had left my keys on her desk. No such luck.

When I dropped into one of Rodney's client chairs, he tore the top page off a yellow note pad and slid it across the desk to me. On it he'd written the name Christopher Woodruff along with a Richmond address on West Seminary Avenue and a phone number. I thanked Rodney for being so quick to get the information for me.

"Well," he said.

"Oh, I know. It'll be on my bill."

"And the phone number is no longer in service," he said.

"So the address may not be good either?"

"According to the Richmond Real Estate Assessor, he still owns the house."

I went back to my office to pack my briefcase, and while I was doing it Brooke stuck her head in.

"You haven't seen my keys, have you?" I asked, looking up. "I can't find them."

"I thought I saw them on your credenza this morning. Where are you going?"

"In search of the person who sent me the handgun."

"Maybe you swept your keys into the trashcan with all the styrofoam peanuts," Brooke suggested.

"Ah hah!" I lifted the trashcan onto the desk. It was nearly half-full of peanuts, but no keys were buried in them.

I sat down.

"What are you going to do?" Brooke asked.

"I have a spare key to my Beetle at home."

"Very useful."

"I don't guess you're ready to leave for the day," I said.

She looked at her watch. "I've got someone coming in at two," she said, sounding regretful. "I don't know how long it'll take." Brooke had started her business about the same time I had, but her business was exploding. Within the year she'd have to hire someone, or she'd be turning away work.

"Maybe I could borrow your car," I suggested.

"Sure. I'm stuck here all afternoon."

Seminary Avenue ran north and south out of the campus of the Union Presbyterian Seminary. West Seminary proved to be a mile or so north of the seminary, where the road split into east and west and the houses got smaller and less majestic. I took the left fork. Christopher Woodruff lived on the left in another half a block. I drew Brooke's Honda CR-V up against the curb opposite the house and got out.

If I had to describe the house, and I guess I do, I would call it a cape cod with Tudor pretensions. Instead of two small dormers, it had a cross-gable on one side with exposed half-timbers. I walked up the flagstone sidewalk. Though it was early afternoon, the sky had clouded up again and already the day was turning brisk.

I rang the bell and waited, hugging myself against the chill. There was no answer. I looked at my watch. It was really too early for anyone to be home from work. I rang again, not hoping for much, then retreated to Brooke's car. I wasn't going to get to talk to Christopher Woodruff, but there were compensations. I had time to go home for my spare car key before heading back downtown.

For a minute or so, though, I sat in Brooke's car, looking at the house and thinking. No point in looking in a window, I told myself, and going through the gate in the chain-link fence to check out the back was probably an equally bad idea. Leave a note. I got a pen and a business card from my purse and wrote, "I have something of yours. Call me."

I looked at it, chewing at the inside of my mouth and wondering if that didn't sound threatening. "I have your gun" wouldn't be any better. I got out another business card and tried again. "Have you been trying to reach me? Robin Starling." Better, though it might look to the state bar as if I were soliciting clients. Certainly I could use a client or two.

I strode back up the walk, my head bent against the freshening wind, opened the storm door, and stuck the card into the crack between the door and jamb. I was halfway down the sidewalk when a small Ford slid up against the curb.

The woman who got out was wearing a bright yellow puff-jacket. She looked at me over the roof of her car, then opened her rear door and leaned into the car. When she straightened, she had a small boy on her hip, a purse on her shoulder, and a couple of grocery bags in one hand.

"Anything I can help with?" I said, approaching her.

"I doubt it." Her voice had a hoarse quality to it, was almost a smoker's voice. She closed the car door with her knee and came around the vehicle.

"I'm Robin Starling."

"Reporter or police?" She barely glanced at me as she passed me on the sidewalk, but her little boy held out a pudgy hand, opening and closing his fingers.

"Hey, there, buddy," I said, waving back at him. "What's your name?"

"Caden Wooruff," he said. "Two burfdays." He indicated the number by extending his index and little fingers.

"Reporter or police?" the woman said more sharply, trying to shift the boy away from me, but hampered by her groceries.

"I'm looking for Christopher Woodruff."

"That's a new one." She stepped onto the stoop and pulled open the storm door, stepping into it and putting down her shopping bags to fumble one-handed in her purse for her keys. I stepped up beside her and held the storm door off her. She glanced again at me as she fitted a key to the lock. The skin around her eyes had a bruised look.

"Why would I be a reporter or police?" I asked.

"Why are you here then?" She pushed open the door and bent for her packages, still balancing the toddler on her hip.

"I guess it wouldn't do any good to repeat that I was looking for Christopher Woodruff." I took the plastic bags from her, and she let me.

"Chris is dead."

"Oh. I'm sorry."

"Sorry doesn't begin to cover it."

"Was he ill?"

"He killed himself."

"Wow."

"The police say it's murder, unfortunately. They couldn't find a gun, and they seem to think I should be able to produce one. Why should I be able to find a gun if they can't?"

If he'd died of a gunshot wound, the absence of a gun at the scene did seem to put the kibosh on her suicide theory, though I didn't like to say so. "I'm Robin Starling," I said again, following her through a living room and dining room with worn wood floors into a kitchen bright with new black-and-white linoleum.

"Yes, you said that. I'm sorry, the name doesn't mean anything to me." She put down her boy, and he clung to her leg.

"You didn't send me a package?"

"I did not." She squared off to face me, her hands on her hips. She was a head shorter than I was and slender, with very pale skin and black hair that swept down over one eye. "What package?" she said, looking up at me. "What's this about?"

I took a breath. "I got a gun in the mail this morning, a small Smith & Wesson semiautomatic. It was purchased by Christopher Woodruff, who listed this address on his registration form."

She continued to look at me, but now her expression was blank.

"Did your husband have a gun?"

She nodded.

14

"I seem to have it now," I said. "It came in a Priority Mail flat-rate box."

"When? Today?"

I nodded. "It came in the mail."

"How well do you know Chris?"

"I never heard the name before today. I'm a lawyer."

"Who sent you Chris's gun?"

"I don't know."

"Why did they send you Chris's gun?"

I shrugged. "No idea."

The fire in her face faded abruptly. She swayed and caught herself on the jamb of the kitchen door. Her boy, looking up at her, had the fabric of her pants leg twisted in his two small fists. I put a hand to her elbow. "Let's go sit down. Can I get you a glass of water?"

She shook her head, but let me lead her into the living room, where she dropped onto the couch and her son clambered onto her lap. "I don't know what to do," she said.

"You could tell me your name," I suggested. "Are you Mrs. Woodruff?"

"Willow Woodruff." She had a tiny mole just off the corner of her mouth, a Marilyn-Monroe-style beauty mark

"Alliterative," I said.

"It's a terrible name. Willow Wendell was bad enough. Willow Woodruff is terrible. I don't know what I was thinking."

"What happened to your husband?"

"He shot himself in our bed Friday morning. Shot himself or was shot."

"Where were you?"

"At work. I'm a COTA at Sheltering Arms. Certified Occupational Therapy Assistant."

"Where was Caden?" I gestured at her son. "Did I get that right? Is your name Caden?"

He nodded. "Caden Wooruff. Two burfdays," he said again.

"Caden was at daycare," Willow said. "I left the house right at seven, dropped him off on my way to work. Chris was still in bed."

"What does he do for a living?"

"Teaches economics at J. Sargeant Reynolds. He'd had a night class the night before, didn't have a class until eleven on Friday. He often sleeps late on Fridays." We were both talking about him in the present tense.

"When did you find out something was wrong?" I asked.

"His dean called me just before noon, his dean's secretary. Chris hadn't shown up for class, and he wasn't answering his cell. He'd given them my cell as a contact for emergencies, evidently. I tried to call him myself, but of course there was no answer. I thought…" She swallowed. "I went home at lunch. The Sheltering Arms is on the Southside, and the drive back and forth was going to take most of my lunch hour, but I thought…" Again she broke off without articulating her thought.

"Chris had some health problems?" I prompted. "You were concerned?"

She shook her head. "He'd been having an affair. I was concerned, yes."

When she didn't go on, I said, "You were thinking that he might have resumed the affair? Or might not have broken it off in the first place?"

No response, just a stricken, far-away look.

"Who had he been having the affair with?"

Her tongue appeared between her lips. She swallowed and started to speak, but had to stop to clear her throat. "Peyton," she said finally. "Peyton Shilling." She sat breathing. "She was in his night class last fall, I think. One morning he ran into her in the weight room at Gold's Gym, and things developed from there. He moved in with her just before the Thanksgiving holiday. It got ugly."

"But he'd moved back home? When?"

"About a month ago. Right after Spring Break, I think. A day or two after."

Sometime in the middle of March then.

"So you went home for lunch and found him in the bed?"

She nodded, miserably. "He was cold. And there was blood, so much…"

I was calculating. Seven to noon might have dropped the body temperature only six or seven degrees, but compared to what you'd expect when you touch someone, the difference would be shocking. "How long had he been dead? Did the police say?"

"About five hours. I got home just before twelve-thirty. They think he died sometime between seven and eight."

"How many times had he been shot?"

"Just the once." She flared briefly. "Nobody shoots himself in the head multiple times."

"No, they don't," I agreed. Most people didn't kill themselves and dispose of the gun afterwards. "Did you see anyone when you left the house that morning?"

"No."

"A car idling across the street maybe?"

"Nothing like that."

"Did Chris have any enemies that you know of?"

She shook her head. "Everybody likes Chris. Liked him." She gave a bitter laugh. "It's me they usually can't stand."

"What's wrong with you?"

"I don't know. I wish I did."

"Do the police have any suspects, other than you?"

"Not that I know of. I told them about Peyton Shilling, of course, but if they followed up on it, they didn't tell me."

"Even if he killed himself, it wasn't just a suicide. Someone was here. Someone picked up the gun and mailed it to me, either after discovering the body or …" I shrugged.

"Or after killing him. So you're thinking you've got the murder weapon."

"I have no way of knowing. It's a heck of a coincidence, if it isn't."

"Nothing coincidental about it. Someone's set this up deliberately."

"Yes," I agreed. "Any idea who?"

"No idea."

"You'd almost think it had to be someone who knows both of us—you and me, or maybe Chris and me."

"I sure don't know you."

"No. I guess you do Facebook?"

"Facebook? Sure."

"I don't, much," I said. "I think I've got fourteen friends."

She snorted. "Fourteen friends. I don't believe that."

"You have more than that?"

"Hundreds."

"If I send you a friend request, will you accept it? I'd like to scroll through your Facebook friends, see if anyone jumps out at me. If I don't recognize anyone, maybe we could try Twitter or Instagram or whatever other social media you keep up with."

"You said you're a lawyer, didn't you?"

"Yeah."

"Do you…help people in situations like this?"

"Sometimes."

"I can't pay you."

"Did your husband have life insurance?"

"Some."

"Then you can pay me. You may not need me, though. Maybe the police will find whoever did this and leave you alone."

I saw in her face that she didn't think so. "Someone told me…" She cleared her throat and started again. "Someone told me that if I'm convicted of killing Chris, I can't…"

"Can't collect anything on the insurance? That's true, but Caden could collect. His finances would be managed by a conservator until he's eighteen—and you're a long way from being convicted of anything."

She took a big breath and let it out slowly. "We'll see."

Caden, activated perhaps by the mention of his name, tugged at his mother's sleeve, and she bent her head toward him.

"Have 'nana?" he whispered in a clearly audible voice.

Willow smiled down into his questioning face. "Sure, honey. You can have a banana."

I followed them into the kitchen, and we talked about who might have a key to their house. There didn't seem to be anyone. As far as she knew, there were just the two keys, Chris's and the one she carried.

"Could I see the bedroom where you found your husband?"

"I guess." She moved toward the door, but Caden squealed and held up his hands to her, one of them clutching the half-peeled banana. She picked him up.

There was a short hall off the living room, at one end of it a bedroom with a full-size bed and a bare mattress.

"This is your bedroom?"

"It was."

"Where do you sleep now?"

She turned and I followed her past a bathroom that might not have been renovated since the house was built in the 1940's or 50's. In a room with a Noah's-ark border around the ceiling, on the floor in the corner opposite a crib, was a twin-sized mattress neatly made up with pin-striped sheets and a navy comforter.

"I see," I said.

"I couldn't bear to sleep in the other room after..." She moved her head, and I nodded.

Before I left, she showed me the only room in the house I hadn't seen, the closed-in porch on the opposite end of the house. Chris had used it as his study. He had a V-shaped computer table in the corner with a computer on it and a two-drawer filing cabinet at one end.

"Maybe at some point I should come back and look through things," I suggested.

"Sure."

"But I guess that's everything right now."

"What are you going to do with the gun?"

"I have to turn it over to the police," I said apologetically. "Does it have your fingerprints on it, do you think?"

"Maybe. When we went to the shooting range, we weren't always particular about who was using whose gun. How long do fingerprints last?"

"Wait. What do you mean, 'who was using whose gun'? Is there another gun?"

"We got matching guns several years ago and went through some kind of course and everything. That was before Caden was born."

"Could I see your gun?"

She shook her head. "I seem to have lost track of it somehow. The police searched the place, and they couldn't find it either."

Chapter 2

The pistol in my desk drawer had gone from being a curiosity to being a potential murder weapon in a homicide investigation. I considered the implications as I headed back downtown with Brooke's car. What I had was a ticking time-bomb, and I didn't know when it was going to go off.

I was going the wrong way. Instead of driving down Chamberlayne Avenue toward downtown Richmond, I should have been kicking out to I-64 and heading home to get the spare key to my VW Beetle. I was distracted enough that I didn't think of that until I was parking Brooke's car along the curb on Jefferson, almost under the giant policeman's head that protruded from the big gray edifice that was police headquarters. Ah, well. I pushed through the revolving doors into the building, put my purse on the conveyor belt to go through the x-ray machine, and walked through the metal detector. Once through, I took the elevator to the fifth floor where the homicide division was located.

The desks were arranged in three rows. A single detective was typing on a computer in a back corner, but he wasn't anyone I knew, and he didn't look up. I stood watching him for maybe half-a-minute, then I stepped back out into the hall. I fished my cellphone out of my purse and found "Jordan"—that would be Police Detective James Jordan—in my list of contacts. My thumb hovered over the screen as I thought about what I was doing. If what I had turned out to be the murder weapon, I could hardly pretend I didn't know whose it was and why the police might be interested in it. In fact, now that I had visited Willow Woodruff, I would never be able to convince anyone the gun hadn't come from her. Keeping the gun was not an option, but turning it over to the police wasn't much better.

The alternative was to do something devious that would put the gun in the police's hands without letting them know it came from me. I punched the button for the elevator while I considered possible options, but unfortunately nothing very clever came to mind. I was a bystander, I told myself. I didn't even have a client, and there was nothing to be gained from taking risks.

The elevator doors opened on an empty elevator, and I stepped on as I tapped Jordan's name. Jordan's name and face filled the screen—close-clipped, graying hair, biker mustache and all. It wasn't a photograph I had taken. I'd copied it from a story the Times-Dispatch had run on Jordan when he'd been shot in the line of duty last summer…okay, when I'd gotten him shot last summer, but there are details one prefers not to dwell on.

"Uh oh" was how he answered the phone.

"Hi, Jordan."

"This can't be good."

I like to think that such pessimism was unjustified, but I said, "I'm calling about Christopher Woodruff. I came by headquarters to see you, but you're not at your desk."

There was a silence.

"Have you heard the name? Woodruff isn't your case, is it?"

"No, it's not my case. I think it might be Tom McClane's. What have you got to do with it?"

Tom McClane, an incompetent jerk in my opinion, was not good news. On the plus side, he was at least a known quantity. "I got a Priority Mail package this morning. When I opened the box, a handgun fell out."

"What kind of handgun? Who sent it?"

The elevator doors opened on the ground floor, and I walked out through the lobby. "A Smith & Wesson of some kind. No idea who sent it. There was no return address, nothing else in the box except a bunch of styrofoam peanuts. Rodney Burns checked on the gun for me—you remember Rodney—and it turned out to be registered to Christopher Woodruff."

"Sounds like you put your foot in it again."

"I didn't put my foot in anything. I opened my mail."

"Of course you did."

My phone beeped, and I glanced at the screen. Brooke Marshall was calling. "Well, I'll try to get hold of McClane," I said.

"I'd do it quickly. You don't want to sit on evidence in a murder case."

"That's why I came straight to police headquarters. It's why I'm calling you."

"Just saying," he said.

"Thanks for the warning."

By the time I signed off, I was out on the sidewalk beside Brooke's car and I'd missed her call. I got into the CR-V and touched her name.

"Robin," she said as she answered.

"Hey, Brooke." I pulled away from the curb. "I haven't been home yet. Do you need your car now, or do I still have time to go get my spare key?"

"Forget it. Carly found your keys. They were in the kitchen next to the coffee maker. You've got bigger problems. The police have been here."

"What? What for?" I turned the car down Cary Street in the general direction of my office.

"They wanted to talk about your morning package, and they didn't seem to like it that you weren't here."

"How do you know what they wanted? They didn't just ask for me and leave?"

"No. They questioned both Carly and me."

"And they asked about my package specifically? They knew what was in it?"

"They knew."

"So what did you tell them?"

"What could I tell them? I'm not in charge of your mail."

"What did Carly tell them?"

"That there might have been a priority-mail box in your mail, but there were a lot of packages today."

I had friends, I'll say that. "I guess that was all she knew," I said.

"Well."

"What do you mean, well?" It didn't matter, of course. I'd just been telling Jordan all about the gun I'd gotten in the mail.

"She heard us talking about it on the way out to lunch, evidently, and later on she button-holed me about it, and, well..."

"Back to well," I said, turning into my parking garage.

"Sorry. I was just thinking about it as a novelty, not something that was going to involve the police and all. Why are the police involved, anyway?"

"It's possible that someone was shot with that gun last week. Did you give it to them?"

"No, of course not. Carly wouldn't even let them in your office. What do you mean someone was shot with it? Who?"

I waited until I got to the office to fill them in, Brooke and Carly and Rodney, keeping the story general enough to avoid any details that weren't public knowledge. I warned them about lying to the police or even withholding information. "I don't want to have to defend you on charges of obstruction of justice."

Carly's eyes had widened alarmingly. "But you would, wouldn't you?" she asked. "Defend us?"

"Of course, she would," Brooke said. "The reason she wouldn't want to is she doesn't feel like she could charge us for it."

"I'm thinking that with a little effort, she could put aside those feelings," Rodney said, and I shot my index finger at him.

"So let's be careful out there," I said.

When Dr. McDermott answered the door in response to my ring, my dog Deeks went streaking past me to do a tight figure-8 on the lawn, his paws throwing up grass clippings as he made the far turn. He came blistering back toward me and dropped into a sit, panting, his tongue lolling and his tail sweeping the front stoop.

"Hey, Deeks," I said, patting his head. "Hey, old buddy."

"You're the only one who calls him that, you know," Dr. McDermott said. "I have to admit that Deacon was a pretty big name when he was a little squirt, but he was sixty-four pounds this morning, and he'll be getting bigger."

Deeks was a labrador retriever whose paws still looked too big for his body. There was little doubt he'd be getting bigger.

"Of course he's your dog," Dr. McDermott said. "We can all call him Deeks if that's his name."

"He seems to do all right with both names. How did you weigh him?"

"I weighed myself, then picked him up and stepped back on the scale."

I was impressed. Sixty-four pounds was a lot of dog. "I won't ask you the combined weight," I said.

He smiled. "I'm an old man. We love to talk about our vital statistics. The combined weight was 238. You can do the math."

"Sound like you're a lean hundred and seventy-four pounds."

"It does sound like that, doesn't it?" He turned sideways to me, pulling in his gut and patting it. Deeks was standing now, his snout jammed between my knees as I scratched vigorously behind his ears.

He fanned the air with the strong, otter-like tail that had cleared my coffee table more than once.

"How was work?" Dr. McDermott asked.

"Same-old-same-old. Problems with the police." I thumped Deeks's side a few times and straightened.

"Want to talk about them?"

I shook my head, smiling. "Not really. I want to take a run before dinner, clear my head."

"You and Deacon have fun."

"We always do."

When we got back from our three-miler, Brooke Marshall was parked by the curb in front of my house. Deeks streaked ahead of me, and Brooke got out hastily so he wouldn't jump up on her car door and scratch the paint again. There were already a couple of scratch marks on the door left by his hard toenails when he'd jumped up on previous occasions to peer in at her. Deeks spun in front of her, about to turn himself inside out in his excitement to see her.

"Hey Deacon," she said reaching into the swirling fur in an attempt to lay a hand on his head. "Hey Deacon, old boy." When he had calmed down enough to accept her ministrations, she scratched his neck and head.

"Does he look more like a Deacon to you, or a Deeks?" I asked.

"He's growing into Deacon."

"That's what Dr. McDermott said. Deacon!"

He turned to look at me.

"Come, Deacon."

He came to me and sat, looking up expectantly.

"In some ways he's very well trained," Brooke said as I scratched his chin.

"And in some ways not?"

"Well, I do have to be careful about him jumping on my car door."

"I wish you'd let me get that fixed."

"Someday maybe. Let's get Deacon through his puppy phase." She reopened the car door and got out her purse and two plastic sacks of sandwiches and chips from Subway.

"You brought dinner."

"A couple of turkey subs. If you've got a bottle of white wine, we're in business."

"We're in business," I said. As we walked up the sidewalk, Deeks—Deacon—bounced beside her, his nose bumping the Subway sacks that dangled from her hand.

When we got to my door, I slipped the string with the house key from around my neck. "I forgot to ask. Did you recognize any of the cops who came by?"

"One of them. I'm pretty sure it was your friend Tom McClane." She went by me, and I closed the door behind us. McClane was in homicide, which meant the police were in my office in connection with someone's death, almost certainly Woodruff's. He was my friend in the sense that he had once hit on me.

"Short, deep-chested guy with a salt-and-pepper flat top?"

"That was him. I hadn't seen the other one before—skinny, blond-haired guy who looked about forty."

"That would be Matt Tarrant, McClane's partner. After we eat, I want to get a pad of paper and get down the exact questions they asked you, as close as you can remember them."

"Oh, I wrote them down." She put the Subway sack on the kitchen table and unzipped her purse to pull out a small pad of paper. "But first, I want to hear more details about this murder. You just showed up at the house, and the widow hired you?"

"Well, no. No client yet, just a murder weapon burning a hole in my desk drawer." I got out stemware and a bottle of Riesling that had been chilling in the fridge. "If it is the murder weapon. So what did McClane ask you specifically?"

She looked at her notepad. "Isn't it true that your friend Robin got a pistol in the mail today, a Smith & Wesson M&P Bodyguard .380 semiautomatic," she read.

That was pretty specific. "And you told him…"

"That I wasn't your secretary, and I didn't open your mail."

"He might take that to mean you didn't know if I got a gun in the mail. If he can later prove you did…"

"I can't be responsible for what he understood. I was careful about what I said, and I made notes. Contemporaneous documentation, isn't it? I haven't spent the last year getting dragged into your cases for nothing."

I started to object to the accusation that I had dragged her into my cases, but immediately thought of several instances where I had done just that.

As she unwrapped her sandwich, Brooke said, "I'm surprised they didn't have a search warrant."

"That's significant, I think. Of course, searching an attorney's office can involve some technical difficulties. More likely, though, is they suspected I'd gotten a gun in the mail, but they didn't have probable cause." I took a bite of my turkey sandwich on 9-grain honey oat.

"And that would mean...what?" Brooke said.

"Most likely that the source of their information was an anonymous tip."

"So they got a phone call."

Deeks was sitting at attention, his eyes on a bit of sandwich wrapper that protruded over the edge of the table. Globs of drool were collecting at the corners of his mouth. Usually, I made him wait until I'd eaten before I fed him—it showed him where he ranked in the pack—but I wasn't as consistent as I should be. I went to the cabinet and scooped a cup of kibble into his bowl.

"Probably it was a phone call," I said. "A letter would have had to have been sent to the police at the same time as the package to me, though I guess that's possible, too."

"In either case, somebody sent you the gun, then tipped the police you had it. Why?"

"I don't know. Maybe just to make trouble for me. Or maybe this someone is involved with Woodruff's murder and is trying to scramble the evidence."

"Woodruff is the man who was murdered."

"Yes, with his own pistol, if what I've got is the murder weapon."

"This someone must know about your history with the D.A."

"Yeah." Aubrey Biggs was not my biggest fan. Actually, Aubrey was pretty convinced I was a crooked shyster. "Certainly he's never going to believe any story I tell about how a murder weapon just showed up in my mail."

"So what are you going to do?"

31

"Get the gun out of my possession just as soon as I can. I've already called Jordan and told him about it."

We were halfway through our sandwiches when Brooke said, "So who do you think called in the tip? You do agree it has to be the same person who sent you the pistol, don't you?"

I swallowed and took a sip of wine. "I think so. The other possibility is that somebody who knew I got one in the mail decided to try to stir something up."

"That would make it somebody in the Executive Suites, and the only ones who knew about it…"

"I'm not willing to go there. It could have been someone who knows the sender, was aware of what he or she was doing."

"Well that means it could have been anybody."

"That's right. We really don't know enough to narrow it down."

We finished our sandwiches. I poured us each another glass of wine to take into the living room. Deeks, who had lain at my feet after he finished his dinner, got up when I did.

"Hey, Deacon," I said, deliberately using his full name. "I'm sorry, buddy. I didn't save you anything."

He wagged his tail, looking back and forth between us.

"I saved him a piece of turkey," Brooke said. Deeks went immediately and took it from her. He glanced at me, then followed Brooke into the living room.

"You're trying to replace me in his affections," I said, trailing after them.

"All I have to do is treat him a little better than you do."

"It was you who called the police, wasn't it? You're trying to get rid of me so you can take my place."

"I'd take Deacon and Paul. I don't know what I'd do with your law practice."

"What about Mike? What would you do with him?"

She sat on the sofa and curled her legs under her. "I don't know. I might keep him, too," she said.

That night Paul called me. I knew who it was before I answered, because the ringtone I'd assigned to him was Bread's "Baby, I'm-A Want You."

"Hello, boo thang," I said. My boo thang was what Brooke called him, I think to annoy me, but I'd picked it up. "You're calling late."

"Are you in bed?"

"About to be." I rinsed the toothbrush I'd just finished using and put it in the drawer.

"I just got off the phone with Mike. He tells me we have competition."

"Ha," I said, walking through the house to check the locks, my dog trailing along behind me.

"You didn't have lunch today with a man named Carter Fox?"

"Not really. It would be more accurate to say Brooke and I walked to and fro with him."

"What does 'fro' mean, anyway?"

"From? I don't know. I've only ever heard it in that one phrase."

"What I heard is that this Carter Fox is a great admirer of all things Robin."

"And all things Brooke. All things female, I suspect." I shucked out of my gym shorts and got into bed, and Deacon—if that was going to be his name now—hopped up beside me.

"So we don't have anything to worry about, Mike and I."

"Well," I said.

"Well?"

"You've never been quite so impressed by the muscle tone in my buttocks. At least you've never told me you were."

"What?"

"Just kidding. I didn't let him touch my butt. Really, he's an annoying man who rented an office in the Executive Suites. There's nothing at all attractive about him."

"You're talking to a two-hundred pound man who's five feet, six inches tall."

"That's right. I'm talking to my teddy-bear boyfriend," I said, snuggling deeper in the covers.

"You're darn tootin'."

"I am darn tootin'," I said.

We talked for probably another twenty or thirty minutes until I was sleepy enough that I kept losing the thread of the conversation. Finally, Paul said, "Robin?"

"Mmm?"

"Go to sleep now. Good night."

"Good night, Pooky," I said comfortably.

"Good night, Garfield."

I clicked off and stretched catlike to put my phone on the nightstand.

It was nine o'clock when I got to work the next morning, about standard for me since Deacon came into my life. Willow Woodruff was in the waiting area. She stood as I pushed through the glass doors into the Executive Suites.

"Where's Caden?" I said, glancing around for him.

"I left him with a neighbor. It's an imposition—he was screaming when I left—so I don't have long."

"Come on back."

Once we'd settled in my office, I said, "You're not working this week, I take it.."

"No. Husband died Friday, I thought I'd take the week off. I want to hire you to represent me in this."

"This what? Have the police charged you?"

She shook her head. "Not yet, but in the meantime there's the insurance." She handed me some papers. "Six hundred thousand in total."

What she had handed me was a policy from Northwestern Mutual and one from Ameritas.

"I think the insurance companies are stalling me," she said.

"It's only been a week."

"I'm thinking about Caden. Somebody's got to look after his interests if something happens to me. Something legal, I mean."

I was looking at the policies. There was no secondary beneficiary for either one, just Willow Wendell Woodruff as primary. "Who owns your house?" I said.

"Why? Is that important?"

"I'm thinking about getting you out on bail if you're arrested. I don't want you to be separated from Caden any longer than necessary."

"Well, well," a voice said from the doorway. "The plot thickens." It was Detective Tom McClane. He'd grown a goatee since I'd seen him last. In contrast to his steel gray hair, it was pure white.

"Hello, McClane."

"I figured Willow Woodruff was your connection to this case."

"What can I do for you? Or did you just drop by to eavesdrop on an attorney-client conference?"

"I came to pick up a murder weapon. I think you know that."

"What makes you think the weapon I have is the murder weapon? Your anonymous tip?"

"What do you know about that?"

"You knew I had a gun, but didn't have enough for a search warrant. That says anonymous tip to me."

"Pretty smart. Too smart by half. As soon as you found out I was here demanding to see this gun, you called Jordan to tell him you had it. You wanted us to believe you were just being a good citizen, but really you were just trying to cover your…" He glanced at Willow. "…cover your backside."

"So you're back with a warrant?"

"Just let me have the gun, Starling."

I took a breath, nodded. "All right." I pulled out the second drawer on the right hand side of my desk. There was no gun.

I pushed the drawer back in and pulled out the top drawer, pushed that one in and pulled out the bottom drawer. Then I started pulling out drawers on the other side.

"This isn't a game, you know," McClane said. Willow Woodruff had stood, her dark hair spilling over one eye, and she stared in what appeared to be

36

horrified fascination. I turned in my chair, my gaze moving from my one set of bookshelves to my credenza, back to my desk.

"So what are you telling me?" McClane asked me. "That you had the gun, but now you've lost it?"

I pulled out the second drawer on the right-hand side again. "It came in the mail yesterday. I put it right here. I haven't opened the drawer since right after lunch yesterday."

McClane moved to where he could look down into the drawer, but there wasn't anything in it at all. Sometimes I kept my purse there, but this morning I'd come in with Willow and just dropped it on the floor up against my credenza.

"Just a minute," I said. "I'll be right back." I turned back in the doorway. To Willow I said, "Don't talk to him. Don't say anything. If he asks you what time it is, you're a deaf-mute."

She nodded, her visible eye open wide. I assume the eye hidden by her fall of hair was open wide, too, but I'm reporting what I saw.

Brooke's door was closed, and I didn't know whether she was in there working or off at a client's. Rodney's door was open. He looked up when I stopped in the doorway, his eyebrows rising.

"Problem?"

"You didn't take that handgun out of my desk for some reason, did you?"

He shook his head.

"Didn't see anybody going in or out of my office?"

"No. I really can't see anything from my desk but that wall." His office was more out-of the-way than either Brooke's or mine.

"Didn't hear anybody out here, today or yesterday?"

"Nothing. I can't even tell you if Brooke's been in this morning. Sorry."

I nodded. When I came out of his office, Brooke was at her door, her keys in hand. Her gaze went from McClane, who had appeared in my office doorway, to me. "What's up?" she said.

"That gun I got in the mail yesterday? It's gone."

"What? No."

"This is quite a little skit you're putting on here," McClane said, "but I'm not buying it. I want that gun."

"No, really? Come on, McClane. You've got to see that I've got nothing to gain by making that gun disappear."

"I don't have to see anything of the sort. I find you conspiring with the chief suspect in this case, and lo and behold the very weapon that might tie her to the crime has gone missing. And we can prove it was in your possession. We can prove it out of your own mouth."

"Yes. As I say, I've got nothing to gain by hiding it."

"Look. If I have to come back, it's going to be with a warrant and some help, and we won't just be searching your office. We'll be going through your home, your car...We'll get a court order to open your safety deposit box, if you have one."

"Somebody took the gun. If you find it somewhere else, it's because somebody took it out of this drawer and planted it there. I have no idea who or why."

"So that's how you want to play it," McClane said. "This is the hill you want to die on."

"Oh, sure," I said. "I'm always looking for a hill to die on."

McClane left. I got Willow to fill out and sign the paperwork that appointed me her attorney in all matters pertaining to the death of Christopher Woodruff and set out a pay schedule. I suspected that she didn't have the cash to pay me outside of the insurance policies, and those wouldn't pay off if she were convicted, but she had what she had.

When she was gone, I called Jordan to twist his ear for ratting me out to McClane. The call went to voice mail, but rather than leave a message, I ended the call and found Ray Hernandez in my list of contacts. He answered.

"You're a persistent thing, aren't you?"

"This is the first time I've called you in a month."

"About two seconds after you tried to get Jordan."

"So he's with you? He didn't answer."

"We were just debating whether we should talk to you."

"I'm glad you decided in the affirmative. I want to take you to lunch."

"Just me, or both of us?"

"Either or both. I've got my tail in a crack."

"That's a poetic way to put it."

"So what about it? You name the place."

There was a silence. Jordan said something I couldn't make out, then Hernandez said something. I waited them out. Finally Hernandez said, "Can you be on Cary Street in about thirty minutes?"

I looked at my watch. "Sure."

"Be on the sidewalk maybe a block down from the Tobacco Company." He ended the call.

Brooke had come into my office and taken one of the client chairs. "Was that Jordan? Is he going to help you?"

"Hernandez. I don't know. It was all very cloak-and-dagger." I told her about them wanting me to be on Cary Street in thirty minutes. "I almost expected him to tell me to come alone."

"Are you scared?"

"Shell-shocked, I think. Yesterday morning everything was calm, blue skies, not a hint of trouble anywhere. Now a murder case I didn't even know about has exploded in my face."

There was an art gallery and a bookstore right next to each other in Shockoe Slip, so at least I could window-shop while I waited. Patricia Cornwell, a one-time Richmond native, had a new book out, and copies of it and most of her backlist filled the bookstore window. I was counting the titles when the familiar Ford Explorer turned the corner and began to vibrate down the sloping cobblestone street. I caught sight of it out of the corner of my eye and crossed the street toward it just as it drew even with me. It stopped. I pulled open the rear door and got in. The Explorer started rolling again.

Hernandez was driving. "Hey, Starling," he said, and Jordan twisted in his seat to look at me.

"Once again into the flames," Jordan said. "There's not another lawyer in this city with your talent for landing in trouble."

"Yesterday morning I was at my desk opening mail," I said. "That's my crime. Why all the intrigue? Why not meet me for lunch?"

"You're radioactive at the moment. Any contact with you that's not strictly adversarial will be regarded as conspiring with the enemy. "

"Well, that's great. I appreciate you risking your careers to meet with me at all."

"So what did you want?"

"You told McClane about me having that gun," I said accusingly. "He knew I'd called you."

"What did you want me to do? You told me you had a gun that might be relevant to McClane's investigation. I called him and told him he might want to swing by to get it."

Okay, so I was being unreasonable. "What are the chances I can get a look at McClane's file in the Woodruff case?" I said.

Hernandez snorted. I waited, then gave up that item on my wish list and went on.

"Somebody notified the police I had a gun in my desk. Before I called you, I mean. Do you have any idea who that somebody was? Or where the call came from?"

They exchanged glances.

"An equally interesting question is where did the call go to," Hernandez said. "Your somebody didn't call the police. He called the D.A.'s office, and Aubrey himself sent McClane hotfooting it over to your office to pick up a murder weapon." Aubrey Biggs, Richmond's vertically challenged, curly-headed district attorney.

Jordan said, "So this somebody seems not only to have known about this gun you had, but also about the animosity Biggs feels for you. He placed his call with the precision of a demolition expert placing his bomb charges to take down a building."

"Now you're the one being poetic," I said drily.

"Thanks. I worked on it on the way over here."

"If the tip came from someone who knew about our mutual disregard, then it was someone with the police or the district attorney's office," I said. "An insider of some sort."

"I don't think you're giving yourself enough credit," Hernandez said.

"You can add to your list of suspects anyone who reads the Times-Dispatch," Jordan added. "Biggs has made some pretty harsh statements about you."

"Add to that, Biggs hasn't looked too good in some of the newspaper accounts of your trials."

"You did say it was a phone call," I said. "It wasn't a message made from letters cut out of a magazine or anything."

Hernandez laughed.

"It was a phone call," Jordan said. "Placed yesterday afternoon from a pay phone at Regency Square Mall."

"If you're imagining some big call-tracing operation, don't," Hernandez said. "The D.A.'s office just checked its phone records."

"I didn't know the mall had a pay phone," I said. "I haven't seen one in forever."

"There're still some out there," Jordan said. "This one's near the food court."

"Did the police dust it for prints? Talk to any of the vendors out there, see if they recognized a photograph of anyone connected with the Woodruff case?"

"You'd have to ask McClane, but I doubt it. Right now the thinking is that the call came from a person doing his civic duty."

"His duty," I said. "It was a man who called."

Again, they looked at each other.

Jordan said, "That was my understanding. I can't say for sure."

"Well, this good citizen, whoever he was, knew I had Christopher Woodruff's pistol. The most likely explanation for that is that he sent it to me. If it was in fact the weapon used to kill Woodruff, then we've got ourselves a prime suspect."

"A person, possibly a man, who was in Regency Square Mall yesterday," Hernandez said. "We've practically got him cornered," Hernandez said.

"A person who is not Willow Woodruff and who has been in my office in the last twenty-four hours," I said.

"Back up. Why do you say that?"

"Somebody took the gun."

"What do you mean, somebody took the gun," Jordan said. "Didn't McClane pick it up this morning?"

"No. He didn't. I opened my desk drawer for him so he could take it out himself, but the gun was gone."

"You didn't just misplace it," Hernandez said.

"I did not."

"Holy crap."

"And then some," I said.

Chapter 3

McClane's partner, Matt Tarrant, stood as I reentered the Executive Suites. He wasn't a tall man, and I could look down at his scalp and thinning blond hair even when he was standing.

"Robin Starling," he said.

"Matt Tarrant. That was fast. Back with a search warrant already?"

He handed me an envelope.

"What's this?"

He didn't answer, but stood waiting as I opened the envelope. It contained, not a search warrant, but a subpoena demanding the immediate production of a Smith & Wesson .380 semiautomatic with a certain serial number. I refolded the document.

"Biggs is playing nice, going the subpoena route first," he said. "You should take advantage of it."

"Sure, why not?" I smacked my forehead with the heel of my hand. "Oh, that's right, the gun has gone missing. McClane should have told you I don't have it anymore. It might have saved you the trip over here."

"You're not doing yourself any favors."

"No, I don't suppose I am."

He left without the gun. It was that or pull out his sack lunch and wait for me to spin copy paper into blued steel. The wait would have been a long one. Rumpelstiltskin I was not.

"Trouble?" Carly said when he had gone.

"Yeah."

"Bad trouble?"

"It's hard to say. I'm not sure what I'm up against."

"You are the coolest cucumber I know. If the police were in and out of here threatening me all the time, I'd be wetting my panties."

I wagged my head. I didn't like the police attention any more than she would—so I did my best not to think about it.

Rodney came through the archway from our cluster of offices and stopped when he saw me. His Edgar-Allan-Poe mug was in his hand, which meant he was probably on his way to the kitchen for coffee. "You talking about the Woodruff case? I may have some more light to shed on that."

I started back with him, but when he cast a wistful eye toward the kitchen, I said, "Let's both go get some coffee. It can't be as urgent as all that."

His face brightened. We got our coffee and went back to his office. His computer was on his desk, and he'd recently connected a second monitor facing the client chairs.

"Have a seat. I'll turn that monitor on for you." The monitor facing me blinked on, he accepted the new settings, then expanded his browser. He was on Instagram, which was showing an electronic poster that read in block letters, "A man doesn't hurt his woman. He always weighs his actions, not wanting to be responsible for her pain." A comment left underneath the poster said, "Emotional blackmail is never pretty."

"What am I looking at?" I asked.

"Your client's Instagram account."

I leaned closer. "She's WittleWombat?"

"Pretty sure."

Willow Wendell Woodruff was a woman who embraced alliteration.

"Now look at this," Rodney said. He opened another tab to show another Instagram account, this one showing a picture of an average looking guy with a very pretty woman with honey-blonde hair and a big chest that seemed disproportionate to her otherwise slender frame. They both looked about thirty. The caption under the photo said, "The love of my life."

"This is Peyton Shilling's Instagram page."

The third side of the triangle, according to Willow. "Peyton Shilling is the blonde?"

"I think so. The man, I think, is Christopher Woodruff."

There was a comment from WittleWombat below the caption: "I don't understand why anyone would be 'the other woman.' It's just another term for slut and home wrecker." Below that was a comment from Peyton.S.Woodruff: "Spoken like a woman who can't hold onto her man."

Rodney scrolled up. A man's right hand lay over a woman's on a white table cloth next to a coffee cup and saucer.

Rodney clicked back to his original tab and scrolled up to show a photograph of Willow

Woodruff in a hospital bed cradling a new-born infant. It had been posted on New Year's Day, and the caption read, "To have and to hold from this day forward." Peyton.S.Woodruff had commented, "Sad to see a grown woman hiding behind a bassinet."

"It's like they're all in middle-school," I said. "Why wouldn't they make their pages private? Why not unfriend each other?"

Rodney shook his head. "I guess you've noticed that Peyton had taken Chris Woodruff's name. Peyton S. Woodruff?"

"They weren't married, were they?"

"No, though Chris did file for divorce about a month before his death."

"I'd like you to get me the paperwork on that."

"Sure." Rodney switched to a third tab, this one to a Facebook page. Chris Woodruff was in a relationship with Peyton Shilling. Willow Woodruff had left the comment, "This is just sick. It turns my stomach." Beneath that, someone named Megan Harris had said, "Who's lonely now?"

"Who's Megan Harris?" I asked.

"Don't know. One of Peyton's Facebook friends." He switched back to the tab for Peyton's Instagram page and scrolled up to a picture of Chris Woodruff sitting between Peyton's feet, the top of her short skirt brushing the top of his head, his eyes cut upward and his tongue showing between his teeth. The caption was "Ticket to Paradise."

There were a string of comments beneath it.

WittleWombat: Home wrecking is the fallback for a hooker who can't get laid.

CWoodruff85: Stop stalking us, Willow.

Peyton.S.Woodruff: Some of us have a life.

WittleWombat: One of you has a wife.

Petyon.S.Woodruff: Don't try to ruin other people's happiness just because you can't find your own.

Peyton's next photograph was a close-up of Willow's face, looking puffy, her eyes squinted. I imagined it had come from the photos on Chris's cell phone and wondered if it had been taken late in Willow's pregnancy. The caption: "Looks unstable, doesn't she?"

Rodney switched back to Willow's Instagram page and scrolled to a wedding photo, her face and Chris's cheek-to-cheek over a cake topped with a miniature bride and groom. The caption: "Till death us do part."

Peyton.S.Woodruff: No wonder he left you, you manipulative bitch.

WittleWombat: Says the painted whore.

CWoodruff85: You need to get over us and get on with your life.

WittleWombat: Caden, too?

"Last one," Rodney said. He switched back to Peyton's page and scrolled up to a picture of Chris and Peyton jogging. He was wearing warm-ups, and she had a jacket on over a T-shirt and shorts.

WittleWombat: You'd better run.

CWoodruff85: My wife is unstable and even dangerous. If you're one of the dozens of people getting messages from her, you should take that into account.

The photograph had been posted just over a month ago. Chris was less than five weeks away from having his brains blown out in the wittle wombat's bed.

I sat back, thinking what any lawyer in my situation would be thinking: Would these posts be admissible at trial? If Willow was charged with Chris's murder and I couldn't keep them out, it was going to be pretty devastating.

"Useful?" Rodney asked.

I nodded. "More useful to the prosecution than to me, but it's better to know than not know."

"I had some free time and thought if I found something useful, I could bill you for it."

"You're a peach, Rodney."

"Would it be convenient to have contact information for Peyton Shilling?"

"I don't know. How much is that going to cost me?"

He stuck a Post-it note on the edge of the desk in front of me. On it were an address and phone number. "It didn't take five minutes. I'll throw it in, gratis."

I picked it off the edge of the desk as I stood.

He stuck another Post-it on the edge of the desk. "Employment information," he said.

I eyed it.

"You can take it. I'll throw that in, too."

I smiled as I took it. "I have to say—and I mean this sincerely—you're worth every penny, Rodney Burns."

Peyton was a yoga instructor at Gold's Gym, which probably explained the muscle definition in the golden legs on prominent display in several of her photographs. I called the number for Gold's on the Post-It.

"Do you have yoga classes for beginners?" I asked.

They did, Monday through Friday at eight a.m.

"Is that Peyton Shilling's class? Someone told me she was really good."

"Yes, it's Peyton's class."

"But it hasn't met the last week or so, I heard. Some kind of personal tragedy?"

"I hadn't heard that. Just a minute." The phone clunked down. There was some background conversation, but nothing I could make out. The voice came back. "The class is meeting regularly. Come any morning."

"Thank you."

Peyton Shilling lived in an apartment in Goochland, about twenty miles out past my neighborhood in Richmond's West End. I could go see her this afternoon, or I could go to her yoga class in the morning. The yoga class would allow for a more casual meeting, but I wasn't sure where it would get me. Would I make friends with her, meet her at a bar, and ply her with margaritas until she started telling me all about her personal life?

Maybe the direct approach.

"Are you wondering how you're going to live until I get back in town?" a voice said from the doorway. It was Paul Soldano. I blinked at him, bringing him into mental focus.

"Isn't it Wednesday?" I said. "Why aren't you still in Norfolk or Lynchburg or wherever?"

"Because I was in D.C. at a conference, not in the hinterlands examining banks. Remember?"

I had a vague sense that I'd heard something about that. "You didn't say anything about it on the phone last night," I said defensively.

"I know. I thought maybe you'd forgotten, and I wanted to surprise you." He held out his arms. "Surprise!"

I went around my desk to give him a hug. We were kind of like Jack Sprat and his wife, except in reverse. I was tall and lean—okay, skinny, if you're being uncharitable—and he was short and chunky. Without going up on tiptoes, I couldn't quite put my chin on top of his head, but I was half-a-head taller.

We hugged, and he patted my fanny, and, because I felt guilty about not keeping track of him better, I let him get away with it.

"That new guy is right," he said. "Like steel cables."

I pulled away from him. "I don't know that comparing my butt to a suspension bridge is a compliment, but I'm going to assume you meant it that way."

"As well you should. What have you got on for this afternoon? Can you take off?"

"I was just heading out to Goochland."

"Oh." He sounded disappointed.

"Want to come?" I asked.

"What's in Goochland?"

"A home wrecker named Peyton Shilling."

"A good-looking home wrecker?"

I caught his nose between my index and middle fingers, and he went still. "Yes, very." I let go of his nose. "Sorry," I said. "Things have me a little on edge." I tried to remember whether I'd said anything to him about the Priority Mail pistol when I had him on the phone last night, decided I hadn't. Somehow news of Carter Fox had moved the pistol off the front page.

"Shall I follow you out?" Paul asked. "We could drop off my car at your place."

That's what we did. He parked his car against the curb in front of my house and walked forward to get into my VW Beetle with me. "Should we pick up Deacon while we're here?" Paul asked. "He likes car rides."

I shook my head. "Deacon can be a handful."

"Wow. You are in a mood."

After we'd gotten back to I-64, riding mostly in silence, Paul said, "You called him Deacon."

"Isn't that his name?"

"Okay."

I was the next one to break the silence. "I got a gun in the mail yesterday. It's turning into a mess."

"Tell me about it."

I did, and by the time we got to Goochland, he knew as much about the situation as I did—which, unfortunately, was little enough..

Peyton Shilling lived on the third floor of a brand new apartment building that you could see from the interstate. We walked up and rang the doorbell, Paul standing back out of view of the peephole. He was breathing harder than he should have been after the climb. Deeks and I—Deacon and I—were going to have to walk him tonight.

The peephole darkened then lightened again, but the door didn't open.

"My name is Robin Starling," I said through the door. "I'm hoping to talk to you about the death of Chris Woodruff."

For several heartbeats there was nothing, and then the door opened. It was the girl in the photographs, wearing what was possibly the same short skirt Chris had been sitting under, his eyes turned upward as he contemplated Paradise. She was younger than I'd thought from the photos, maybe no more than twenty-five or twenty-six.

"Oh," she said when she saw Paul, and she closed the door again until it was only open about a foot, her toe wedged against it on the inside.

I looked back and forth between them. "You know each other?"

Paul gave his head a quick shake.

"I never saw him before," Peyton said. "I just thought you were alone."

"Paul Soldano," he said and stepped forward with his hand extended.

She looked at it through the narrow opening, and he dropped it to his side.

"Are you police?"

"Not me," Paul said. "I'm this woman's bodyguard, gofer, and all-round dogsbody."

"How about you?" she said to me. "Are you police?"

I shook my head. "Lawyer."

She looked back at Paul. "What's a dogsbody?"

"I'm not sure I know. I think it's the guy who does all the scutwork."

She cut her eyes toward me again.

"Don't ask him what scutwork is," I said. "The explanation will only introduce yet another word to our vocabulary."

"Who's your client?"

"Willow Woodruff."

Her lip curled. "The grieving widow. She's been arrested then?"

"No. Not yet."

"She will be. She should be."

"You think she killed her husband?"

"Of course." After a moment she gave a small nod, as if to herself, and stepped back from the door. "Come in."

We followed her in.

"Have a seat."

We sat, me on the sofa, John in an armchair, but Peyton remained standing, her arms crossed beneath her breasts. I'd have liked to know what kind of bra she was wearing and where she got it, but I didn't know her well enough to ask for clothing tips. Instead I said, "What makes you so sure Willow killed her husband?"

"She's unstable. And she'd threatened him."

"What did she say?"

"That she'd kill him before she'd let him go."

"Was he going somewhere?"

She dropped her arms. "He'd moved in with me. Didn't she tell you?"

"Yes. She also said he'd come back."

Peyton snorted, and, coming from her golden face, the sound was unexpectedly porcine. "She would say that."

"He died in her bed," I said.

"Easy enough to undress him and put him there after she shot him."

"What was he doing at the house, then, do you think?"

"He had his stuff there, didn't he? Had a young son even. And it was his house. Her name wasn't even on the deed."

I nodded. "You and he were still together then?"

"We loved each other."

"When did you last see him?"

"Last Wednesday. Two days before he was murdered."

"And you were still together? Where did he spend Wednesday and Thursday nights?"

"How would I know? He stayed here most nights, but he was a free agent."

"I guess he kept some of his stuff here—a change of clothes, a toothbrush?"

"Sure."

"May I see them?"

"I don't think I caught your name. You said Robin…"

"Starling. Like the bird."

"Uh huh. And what makes you think you can walk into people's homes and start taking inventory?"

It was an unexpected turn of phrase for a yoga instructor. I said, "Where did you see Chris last Wednesday night? Here, or at the college?"

"Both. I'm in his economics class."

"And he came back here after?" When she didn't say anything to that, I added, "You were in a class of his last semester, too, weren't you?"

"What of it?"

"Does he take your yoga class? Is it a reciprocal sort of thing?"

Her eyes narrowed. "You've done your research on me, haven't you?"

"Cherchez la femme," Paul said, and she looked at him.

"What?"

I was thinking the same thing: What?

"Look for the woman," Paul said. "It's an expression."

"I think I'd like you to leave now."

Paul had effectively closed down the interview for me. "Is there anything you want to get off your conscience first?" I said.

"What do you mean?" she asked. "Why should anything be on my conscience?"

"You did seduce another woman's husband."

"She didn't own him. Any woman who can't hold onto her man doesn't deserve him."

"So if he'd left you to go back to his wife, that would have hit you pretty hard," I said. "It would have been your fault."

"He didn't leave me. I told you that."

"Had he given you a handgun?" I hadn't moved from the couch.

"No he had not given me a handgun. Why would he do that?"

"Might be worried about your safety."

"Well he wasn't. I can take care of myself. Are you going to leave now, or do I have to call the police?"

I stood, smiling. "No need. Sorry I touched a nerve."

"You didn't touch a nerve. I just don't see any reason to stand here listening to your insinuations."

I turned back at the front door, my hand on the knob. "Maybe you went to his house last Friday morning, maybe you thought it would be a blast to have sex with him in his wife's bed, but he was dead when you got there. You picked up the gun that was there and took it with you."

She took a step toward me, and Paul stepped between us. "You're insane."

"You sure you've never heard my name before? You didn't send me a pistol?"

"Get out."

I pulled open the door and stepped through it. Paul stopped in the doorway, looking over his shoulder at Peyton. In sepulcher tones he said, "Cherchez la femme."

She kicked his shin. He staggered as she connected, but stayed in the doorway. He raised his arms and said it again. "Cherchez la femmmme."

She rushed at him, catching him in the chest with both hands and driving him through the doorway. I caught him, steadying him, and the door slammed.

He looked at me sheepishly. "Sorry. I messed that up for you, didn't I?"

"No, it went about as well as I expected."

"You're kidding."

He followed me down the steps, but he was holding onto the railing and favoring his right leg. When we got to the bottom, I asked him, "What in the world made you start saying 'Cherchez la femme' over and over again like some kind of boogeyman?"

He shrugged. "I developed a sudden dislike for Peyton Shilling."

"She's gorgeous—you see that, don't you? Doesn't it take a while for a man get past that?"

"It's worse when they're gorgeous," Paul said.

"How is it worse? Isn't beauty always a good thing?"

"Not when the inside is ugly. Then the outer beauty's just a mockery."

I beeped my car door unlocked, and he opened it for me. I sat and looked up at him. "You're deeper than I thought," I said.

"Still waters," he said. He shut the door and limped around the car.

When he got in on his side, I said, "I never noticed you being especially still except when it came to exercise."

"I was referring to my inner serenity," he said.

We parked my car in the garage and walked through the house and across the street to pick up Deacon from Dr. McDermott.

"At least you've stopped limping," I said.

"I'll be all right. I may have a bruise."

As we headed home with Deacon, he ran ahead of us across the street.

"Do you even own a leash?" Paul asked me.

"You need to get back in touch with your inner serenity. And, yes. I've got one somewhere."

"You can be serene and curious at the same time." After a moment Paul added, "I am worried he's going to get hit by a car someday."

"He's pretty good about watching for cars."

"He's a dog. Suppose a squirrel comes along?"

"That's why I've stopped listening to music when I run," I said.

"I don't follow."

"I know he can get into trouble off-leash, so I try to keep my own distractions to a minimum."

"If you say so. I'll go back to being serene."

I caught his hand, and we crossed the street swinging our hands between us.

When I'd unlocked the door, Deacon pushed into the house, but stopped as we came in behind him, the fur bristling in a ridge along his spine. He emitted a low growl, and I froze, my hand on Paul's arm, listening.

There was no sound other than the rumble coming from Deacon's chest, not even the hum of the air handler. No sound even from our breathing.

Deacon broke as I was stepping out of my shoes, his toenails slipping on the wood floor as he surged forward.

"Baseball bat in the closet," I called over my shoulder as I ran after him, snatching up a brass duck from an occasional table as I ran by it. Deacon hit the side of the archway as he made the dogleg into the hall on his way to my bedroom, and I slammed into the archway right behind him, glancing toward the guest bathroom and front bedroom as I followed him into mine.

Deacon had stopped, his fur still bristling, his head moving from side to side. He glanced over his shoulder at me, his eyes questioning, as Paul pushed past me into the bedroom, holding the baseball bat in a two-handed grip. The bat was a battered Louisville Slugger that had been my brother's practice bat in high school. Faded black duct tape wound round and round the barrel.

The top drawer of my dresser drawers was open, and lingerie spilled out of it. One pair of panties hung from the knob, another was half off the top of the dresser, several were on the floor. A lacy bra was draped on the shade of the table lamp that sat on the dresser. Another bra, a pedestrian beige-colored one, was hooked to the curtain hooks and stretched across the window.

The door to the master bathroom was closed, the door of the walk-in closet half-open. I jerked my head in the direction of the walk-in closet and moved barefoot to the bathroom door. I turned the knob quietly and, as Paul swung into the closet doorway, pushed open the bathroom door and stepped back. Deacon slipped past me into the bathroom.

"Deacon!"

He turned back, and, for the first time since we'd entered the house, his tail wagged. I felt the tension wash out of me.

"Come, Deeks. Here, boy."

He came out and put his head against my thigh. I scratched his ears as I caught my breath.

"I'll do a quick walk-through," Paul said, and left the bedroom, still holding the baseball bat high.

"Go with Paul," I told Deacon, giving him a nudge with my knee.

When they came back, I was sitting on the side of my bed, gazing at my scattered underwear.

"There's a broken pane in one of your French doors," Paul said. "We must have missed it when we walked through the house on our way to get Deacon."

"So that's how they got in."

"Maybe not."

I looked at him.

"Come see."

The French doors were in the living room at the back of the house. The broken pane was by the door lever, but almost all of the glass was outside on the cement patio, only a shard or two lying near the door on the inside.

"Why would they have broken the window if they were already inside the house?" I asked. "And how did they get in anyway?"

Paul shook his head. "It's nothing obvious. You don't have a key hidden outside somewhere, do you?"

"No. I gave it to you, remember?"

"Maybe whoever it was had an electronic pick gun? Or a bump key? We've seen this kind of thing before."

"Why would anyone break into my house to go through my underwear drawer?"

"Looking for something?"

"*Looking for something* doesn't explain one of my bras stretched from curtain hook to curtain hook."

"No, it doesn't explain that. We need to walk around, see if we can tell what's missing."

It seemed logical to start in the bedroom. I gathered up my underwear for the laundry hamper, not planning to wear any of it again before washing it. When I went to close my dresser drawer, I found myself looking down at a small to medium-sized pistol.

"Uh oh," I said.

Paul came over to look. "That isn't the…" He didn't finish the question, but he didn't need to.

"It looks like it," I said.

"That's not good."

"No, it's not." I was under a subpoena to turn over a Smith & Wesson semiautomatic, which I had been at some pains to deny having. If I tried to explain someone breaking into my house to plant a gun that he or she had stolen from my office, nobody was going to believe a word of it. It didn't make any sense, and my only supporting evidence was a window pane that had been broken from the inside. I imagined myself explaining that I was not that stupid, that if I had wanted to stage a break-in, I would have done a better job of it.

Of course, I could stage a break-in now and do a better job of it, but the district attorney already thought I was in the business of manufacturing evidence. If I actually started doing it, I'd be heading down a slippery slope.

"Crap," I said. "Any credibility I had with the D.A.'s office or the police is now shot."

"Did you have any credibility with the D.A.'s office?"

"Well, no. I did have a little with the police, at least with Jordan and Hernandez."

"So you don't think they'll buy this story?"

I thought about it, then shook my head. "They'll think I'm playing some kind of deep game. Especially…" I broke off. "Let's take a closer look at that gun."

I got a pencil and stuck it in the barrel to lift the pistol from the dresser drawer.

"M&P Bodyguard 380," Paul said, tilting his head to read along the barrel. I turned the gun, and he read, "Smith & Wesson, Springfield, MA, USA," from the other side. "Is it the same gun?" he asked.

"It's the same model. I'll have to check with Rodney about the serial number."

"I don't see the serial number."

We found it in a little slot on the right side of the gun and wrote it down. After we'd dropped the gun into a clear gallon storage bag, I got Rodney on his cell phone, and he confirmed it: This was the same gun I'd gotten in the mail the day before. Christopher Woodruff's gun.

"Why did you think it might not be the same gun?" Paul asked. We were sitting side by side on the living room couch, him with a bottle of the dark beer he liked, me with a glass of merlot. Deacon was sitting against me on the side opposite Paul, his eyes rolled up to watch my face.

"A gun that keeps appearing and disappearing?" I said. "Why would it be the same?"

"How many M&P Bodyguard 380s could there be floating around your home and office?"

"Possibly two." I told him about Willow Woodruff's gun, which neither she nor the police could find.

"Same model?"

"She and Chris got them at the same time. Evidently, target practice and qualifying for concealed carry was an activity they took up as a couple."

"I would think maybe dance lessons," Paul said.

"All couples are different." I turned my head to look at him. "You'd like to do dance lessons? Isn't that too much like exercise?"

"Yes, but there'd be compensations."

"What kind of compensations?"

"Do I have to draw you a picture? I'd be moving around pressed up against you for an hour or so each week. I could get into that."

I patted his leg.

"And we'd have to practice. I'm not all that graceful, you know. We might have to practice a lot."

"You're sweet."

"And kind of horny."

"Well, sure. That goes without saying." We sipped our drinks, and I stroked Deacon's fur.

"Probably this is a bad time to bring this up, because you'll think I've got an ulterior motive—but you know I'm staying here tonight."

"What for?"

"What do you mean, what for? Somebody's been walking in and out of your house. I'm not leaving you alone."

"I won't be alone." I lifted Deacon's chin and looked from his face with its upturned eyes to Paul's.

Paul wasn't satisfied. "No, you won't be alone, because I'll be here with you."

I nodded. There was an air of creepiness in my own house that even Deacon's presence wasn't enough to dissipate. "Do we need to go to your apartment to pick up some stuff?"

"I haven't been home since the D.C. trip. All my stuff is in my car."

"You've got an extra set of underwear?"

He moved his head equivocally.

"Gross," I said.

"Or I could wear some of yours."

My hand closed on a throw pillow and swung it across my body to catch him on top of his head. Paul flinched, but too late to protect himself. Deacon was on his feet and in my lap.

Probably I had overreacted. Certainly it seemed that way as we were blotting my carpet and one sofa cushion with a mixture of dishwashing liquid and hydrogen peroxide in an effort to clean up the spilled beer and red wine.

There'd already been too much weirdness with regard to my underwear for one day, though.

Chapter 4

The next morning, I took the stairs to the second floor of the Ironfronts, the building that housed my office. When I pushed through the glass doors of The Executive Suites, Matt Tarrant stood up, and Tom McClane turned away from the big painting opposite the receptionist's counter.

"It's got a frame on it, so it must be art," McClane said.

"What's up?"

"Got a search warrant for your office. Our instructions were to serve it on you personally." His sneer showed me his upper teeth. "Some kind of claptrap about attorney work product or professional courtesy or something."

Matt Tarrant said, "We weren't gonna wait forever, though. We just called in for further instructions, and Biggs said at nine o'clock just serve it on your receptionist and go on in."

I looked at my watch. It was eight forty-five. "I'm glad I got here fifteen minutes short of forever," I said. "Saves us all a bit of trouble." I put my briefcase on the arm of the sofa and reached into it for the plastic baggie with the handgun.

McClane's eyes widened when he saw it. "Son of a bitch," he said. "You had it all along."

"Unfortunately not. Whoever took it from my office yesterday broke into my house and left it in my underwear drawer."

Tarrant looked from McClane to me. "Do you believe this? Why not just tell us the tooth fairy left it under a cabbage leaf in your backyard?"

It seemed to me he was mixing his folk tales, but I just gave him a perfunctory smile as I handed him the baggie.

"Did you call in the burglary?" McClane asked me.

"No, I didn't see the point. Whoever broke in staged it so it looked staged."

"What the hell does that mean?"

"A glass pane was broken, but the glass was on the outside of the house."

"Matt's right. You tell the damnedest stories. Don't think we're buying any of it."

"I'm not asking you to buy it."

"Good, because we're not."

In the end they took the gun and left. Rodney's door was open and Brooke's wasn't, I noted as I unlocked the door of my office. I dumped my purse and briefcase, grabbed my coffee mug, and went to the kitchen to pour myself a cup.

Carter Fox came into the kitchen behind me, also with a mug in his hand—a black, red, and yellow mug shaped like Mickey Mouse's head. Somehow it didn't surprise me.

"Sounded like the cops were giving you a bad time," he said.

"Oh, not really. They like to pull my chain from time to time."

"They were here about thirty minutes before you got here, demanding to see you, calling in for instructions and everything. It was a lot of excitement for us ham-and-eggers." He laughed. Since I was holding the carafe, I poured his coffee before putting the carafe back on the burner. When I headed back to my office, he followed, his head bobbing agreeably.

"You had a gun they wanted, evidently. It sounded like you've been playing hide-and-seek with it."

"Where were you that you were able to hear all that?" I asked.

"I was in the kitchen awhile, walked back and forth to my office a couple of times. That one officer has a voice that really carries."

"He certainly does." I sat behind my desk despite a vague concern that Carter would take it as an invitation to take a seat himself. He did just that, kicking back in one of my client chairs.

"McClane, isn't it?" he said. "And this time he got what he came for."

"What kind of law do you practice?" I said. "Real estate, wills and trusts, something like that? I don't think I've ever seen you around the courthouse."

"Oh, a bit of this and that. Paperwork, mostly. I'm not a gladiator like you. I consider you in the upper echelon of criminal defense attorneys."

The high praise was undeserved. I'd been out on my own a few months and was only just beginning to feel like I could make a go of it. "I think of myself as a trial lawyer. Criminal defense is what's come through the door lately."

"You've burst on the scene like a shooting star."

I smiled, a little sourly. Carter Fox was a man who could make a compliment feel like a tongue bath.

"I don't suppose you'd care to fill me in on this latest imbroglio. I'd love to hear about it."

Imbroglio. There was a word you didn't hear every day. "Better not," I said. "Client confidentiality and all that."

"I understand. We're their champions in the joust. Their interests come first."

I tried not to roll my eyes. In the end I had to get rid of him by heading for the ladies' room. He followed me down the hall.

"Are you and Brooke Marshall going to lunch again today?"

"Maybe. Us and a couple of others."

"Guys or gals? Don't tell me if you don't want to. It's not really any of my business."

"Guys probably," I said. "Both our menfolk are back in town."

"Ah, yes. Brooke has that fiancé, and you've got the boyfriend. Perhaps not as serious as Brooke's relationship with her gentleman, but there it is all the same."

It was a long hall, and we were only halfway along it, Carter Fox still trailing after me.

"Do you see other people occasionally, or is it more serious than that?" he asked.

Good grief. "It's pretty serious. I tried going out with another guy once, but his body was found in a dumpster the next morning."

"Ah ha ha! Like that, is it? Serious as a heart attack! Jealous boyfriend. I understand that. I actually do."

We had at last arrived at the door of the ladies' room. "So to keep Paul out of prison and other men out of dumpsters, I've curtailed my social life a bit. It's not so bad." And I escaped through the door into the smell of disinfectant.

Carter Fox, to his credit, didn't follow me in.

I did eat lunch with Paul and Brooke and Mike McMillan. It was a beautiful spring day, already in the seventies by lunchtime. We bought sandwiches and carbonated limeades in the basement of the Capitol building and ate on the grounds, sitting on a blanket Brooke had brought. "You engaged people are always thinking up nice occasions like this," I said to Brooke.

She gave me a look that Mike noticed.

"Or was this your idea?" I asked him.

"We talked about it. Sometimes it's hard to tell where my ideas leave off and hers begin."

"Oh, please," Brooke said.

"She's almost giddy in love," Mike said. "You can tell."

"The only thing that makes her grouchier than having a man in her life is not having one," I said.

Paul stood up and sat down again, which distracted us from our observations about Brooke in love.

"What was that about?" I asked him.

"I just thought it needed to be done."

"Either he wasn't getting enough attention, or he had a wedgie," Mike said.

Paul ignored him. "So," he said. "The police came and got the gun." Despite what I'd said to Carter Fox

69

about client confidentiality, all three of them knew all about the migratory handgun.

"Yes, and I'm glad to be rid of it," I said. "Next time it goes missing, it'll be someone else's responsibility."

"So you're in the clear now. It's over."

"Well, maybe. There may be a trial at some point. In the meantime, it looks like I've been playing hide-the-ball with the evidence in a murder case. I doubt Aubrey can prove anything, but I'm sure he'll think the worst."

"I don't know how these things keep happening to you," Mike said. "I've been practicing law as long as you, and no one's ever threatened to bring me before the Disciplinary Board. I doubt Aubrey Biggs even knows my name."

"I can't imagine how it keeps happening. It just does," I said. "And I practice law as conservatively as anyone."

There was a silence.

"What I mean is, I don't try to push the boundaries of professional ethics," I said.

I got some nods with that one. "I'll give you that," Mike said. "That's why I really don't understand it."

"She's a lightning rod," Brooke said. "I think it's because she's utterly fearless."

I rolled my eyes. "Here, let me strike a pose for you."

"I think it's because of her looks," Paul said. "She's like a Valkyrie. She's got the height, the long blonde hair, the athletic build…"

"Oh, come on," I said, dropping the pose. "Stop being ridiculous."

"You don't think your looks attract trouble?" Mike asked.

"Let's go back to talking about you and Brooke. It was a lot more fun."

"No, I like this," Brooke said. "Could you strike that pose again for us? I think we have a few more comments to make about your athletic build. Between the three of us, we might even out-do Carter Fox."

I felt myself turning red, so I took a bite of my sandwich and chewed without looking at anybody.

"Robin Starling speechless," Mike said. "That's a first."

So lunch turned out to be more of an ordeal than it should have been. Afterwards, we all walked back to the Ironfronts. Brooke and I went up; Mike and Paul went on. Once in my office, I looked over what I had to work on, pushed the files aside, and began a vicious game of Spider Solitaire on my laptop.

I lost. I pushed back in my chair, staring blankly at the intransigent columns of cards, my mind back on Willow Woodruff and her problems. The current lull was only temporary. The police would do a ballistics test to confirm that Chris's gun was in fact the murder weapon. They would check for fingerprints, and if they found Willow's, they'd arrest her. Even if the gun had been wiped clean—which I expected—the odds were they'd arrest her anyway. I should be getting a call by the end of day. I ought to warn her.

I picked up my phone and dialed her cell. Just when I thought the call would go to voicemail, she answered.

"Hi, Willow. Robin Starling. Have you seen the police today?"

"No. Should I expect to?"

"There have been a few developments regarding your husband's handgun." I told her about them.

"I don't get it," she said. "Why does this gun keep coming back to you? What have you got to do with anything?"

"Nothing until a couple of days ago. Now, of course, I'm representing you."

"You know who's behind it, don't you?"

"Peyton Shilling?"

"I don't know how she's doing it or why, but she's involved some way," Willow said.

"You may be right." *Cherchez la femme*, Paul had said, and maybe I hadn't been cherchezing enough.

Rodney was in his office. He was kicked back with his Edgar Allan Poe mug clasped in both hands, steam rising from the mug, a look of placid contentment on his face.

"I know you don't do that gumshoe, shadowing people kind of stuff," I said.

"What do you mean? I can shadow people. This is a full-service detective agency. What do you need?"

"Do you do it all yourself, or are there people you use for various kinds of work?"

"I mostly do it myself, but I've got friends I can call on if I get stretched too thin."

I hadn't really thought of Rodney Burns as a man with friends, but I guess we all had them. "Friends in the detective business, or just friends who are willing to pick up a few extra dollars for a job here and there?"

"Both. If it was a sensitive matter, I wouldn't use anybody I hadn't used before."

"I'm thinking I'd like to know a lot more about Peyton Shilling," I said. "Not just background stuff. I think I'd like to track her movements for a while."

"That can be done." He pulled over a legal pad. "So. You want her shadowed 24-7, you just want to know how she spends her evenings, what?"

"Evenings might be enough. That would be cheaper, wouldn't it?"

He nodded vigorously. "A lot cheaper."

I stopped short as I came out of Rodney's doorway. The curly headed hobbit who served as Richmond's district attorney was standing in the archway of exposed brick that opened out into the reception area.

"Aubrey," I said, surprised.

"I think we need to talk." Tom McClane was there, too, standing just behind him.

"The three of us?" I got no answer, shrugged. "Come on in."

I walked around my desk, gesturing to the client chairs. Aubrey sat. McClane closed the door and took the other chair.

"Okay," I said.

"You're a young lawyer," Aubrey said. "A very promising young lawyer with some excellent courtroom skills, but a young lawyer all the same, one without a lot of experience in criminal defense. Is that fair?"

"Maybe," I said.

"It's why I'm here. Criminal cases, murder cases especially, are very serious matters. A life has been taken, the accused faces the possibility of life imprisonment, maybe even execution."

"I kind of understand the general nature of a murder case," I said.

He took a breath. "When your client gives you a murder weapon, you can't just make it disappear."

"No, of course not."

"You can't juggle it around, dumping it out of a Priority Mail box, putting it in a drawer, taking it out again, carrying it around in your briefcase."

"Look. Every time I've seen that gun, I've tried to unload it. I don't mean unload it. I've tried to give it to the police. It shows up in my morning mail, I call the police. It shows up at my house, I put it in a baggie, and I bring it to the police. When…"

"You can't switch guns," Aubrey said heavily.

I looked back and forth between them. "Switched what guns?" I said.

Aubrey's eyes cut toward McClane, then came back to me. "Don't play the innocent," he said. "We know what happened."

"I don't."

"The gun you gave us is Christopher Woodruff's gun."

"Yeah," I said. "That's the gun that keeps showing up."

"We want the gun that fired the bullet that killed Christopher Woodruff."

"Chris's gun wasn't it?"

"The playacting doesn't become you."

McClane said, "Willow Woodruff and her husband purchased identical handguns two years ago last May. You knew that."

I inclined my head. "Willow told me."

"The gun that fired the fatal bullet was the same make and model as the one you gave us," McClane said. "It was a .380 semiautomatic made by Smith & Wesson, an M&P Bodyguard. But it wasn't the same gun."

Aubrey said, "We want Willow Woodruff's gun."

"I don't have it."

"I don't want to parse words with you. Are you saying you've never had it, never seen it, that you don't know where it is?"

"That's what I'm saying."

Aubrey shook his head. "As I understand it, the two guns are identical. How would you know which one you were looking at?"

"This M&P Bodyguard has turned up twice and only twice. Fortunately, I wrote down the serial number the first time. When the gun turned up again, I checked its serial number against the first one. I can swear I have never been in possession of any gun except Christopher's."

Aubrey stood. "If you're lying, it's obstruction of justice."

"If I'm not, it isn't."

He was looming over my desk, in so far as a man who's less than five-and-a-half-feet tall can loom.

I said, "How do you know Willow's gun was the murder weapon? Will you tell me that?"

"Because the Christopher gun isn't."

"How do you know either gun was the murder weapon?"

"We don't know of a third gun of that make and model," McClane said from his seat. "Do you?"

"Surely you're not about to introduce one," Aubrey said.

"No. As I've said, I just seen the one. It occurs to me, though, that Smith & Wesson probably made more than two guns of that model."

"Is that really the way you want to play this?" Aubrey said. "I can promise you it won't go well."

I stood myself so that I was looking down again. "If you can prove I was ever in possession of Willow Woodruff's handgun, then you go for it."

"I made the trip across town to your office today because I wanted to give you a break. You need to take it."

"I don't have the gun you're asking for," I said, speaking slowly, so as to emphasize each word. "I don't know where it is."

"It's not back in that desk drawer of yours?" McClane asked, gesturing with a hooked finger.

My eyes cut toward the drawer. With a sudden sick dread, I knew that was just where Willow's M&P Bodyguard was.

"Well?" Aubrey said, noticing my hesitation.

I took a breath and sat to reach for the drawer. Both men leaned over my desk. My hand touched the drawer, and I stopped. If I opened the drawer and the gun was there, my credibility was shot forever. Possibly, my legal career was over. I considered: I could order them out of my office, but if I did that, my credibility was shot whether the gun was there or not. I looked up at them. We all seemed to be holding our breaths.

I pulled open the drawer.

My purse was there, but otherwise the drawer was empty. I exhaled, and McClane fell back into his seat. Aubrey remained standing.

"You're not just putting your law license at risk," he said. "I will be filing a complaint with the Disciplinary Board, but it won't begin there, and it won't end there. You have taken possession of a murder weapon in an ongoing investigation, and you have failed despite repeated requests to turn it over to police. Now, you've tried to confuse the facts by substituting guns. This makes you an accessory-after-the-fact in a murder case, and I will be charging you as such."

"There're a lot of things you're going to have to prove to make that stick."

"Don't think I can't do it."

"As of right now, you can't even prove that Willow's gun is the murder weapon."

"I can see I've wasted my time coming over here."

"I can see that you did," I said.

I remained standing as they walked stiff-backed from my office. When they disappeared through the archway, I slumped back in my chair. I'd feel better if all this trouble was the result of something I was doing, but it was not. Someone with access to both my office and my home was moving guns around like a con man in a shell game. One instant the gun was under one shell; the next it was under another.

A sick dread settled in my abdomen as I thought about it. The people in the best position to pull off a shell game like this were my friends. Paul and Brooke and Dr. McDermott each had a key to my house, though neither had a key to my office. Carly had a master key that opened my office, but didn't have a key to my house. Brooke's office was close enough to mine for her to monitor my comings and goings, and I didn't lock my door, didn't even close it, when I was on the floor. Rodney's office was close, but it didn't have a line of sight to the archway. He couldn't see me coming and going, and to get to my office he'd have to pass Brooke's. When she was here, her door was usually open, but of course she wasn't always here...

I tapped a finger on the desk. I trusted all of them completely. Suppose, though, one of them had a connection with Chris Woodruff? Would I still trust them completely? Such a connection, undisclosed, would open up some sinister possibilities. I pulled over my laptop and looked up Willow on Facebook again. No need to befriend her to scroll through her list of friends. It was all open to the world. The same was true of Chris Woodruff and Peyton Shilling. It took a bit over an hour to look through all of their friends and photographs. Peyton had the fewest friends, only 87 of them, but the most selfies. None of her self-photos were pornographic, but a number of them were sexually suggestive. Peyton clearly thought a lot of Peyton.

The good news, if it was good news, was that I didn't see any names I recognized, and as I got close to the end of the search, I began to feel a relaxing of the knot in my gut. Finally, I pushed the laptop away and took a few deep breaths. I could never tell Paul or Brooke or any of them that I'd gone looking for them.

I stood up and shook out my arms, then raised my knees a few times to stretch out my buttocks. I was done investigating my friends. Of course, I hadn't actually been investigating them, just the principles in the case. No. I knew what I'd been doing, who I'd been looking for.

I sat. What I could do, without being an overly suspicious paranoiac—if that's not redundant—was continue to investigate Chris Woodruff, the dead man himself. Find out everybody he had associated with in any capacity, no matter how remote. One thing was sure. I didn't have any more time to indulge in Spider Solitaire.

I used my computer to look up J. Sargeant Reynolds, the junior college where Chris Woodruff had taught. It had three campuses, one downtown and two out in the general direction of my home. East Parham Road looked like the main campus. At any rate, it was where the business school was located, and Christopher Woodruff was listed as an assistant professor of business. The dean of the business school, pictured on an inside page, was a big, dark-haired woman named Dr. K.O. Walker. Karen? Kaci? Kelsey? I wondered if she really went by K.O. I picked up the phone to call Dr. Knock-Out Walker, hesitated, and put it back down.

It took me thirty minutes to get to my car and drive out there. There were trees everywhere, a few pines, but most with the bright green growth of spring. The school's parking lot was vast, but I was able to park close enough to the buildings that I exchanged my sneakers for the pumps in my shoe bag to walk to the closest one.

The dean of the business school wasn't in that building, but she was in the next. Her secretary, visible through the sidelight by the door, was a strawberry blonde who looked about twenty. I opened the door and went in.

"May I help you?" She smiled up at me, her head tilted back.

"I don't know. My name is Robin Starling. I was hoping to talk to the dean."

"Dr. Walker? I'll see if she's in."

My eyebrows went up. Through an open doorway I could see a big woman in a plaid jacket working at a big oak desk, but the girl picked up the phone and punched a button. The phone in the inner office gave a soft trill, and the woman at the desk reached out to press something.

"Yes?"

I could hear her through the doorway. She had a deep, foghorn sort of voice, not unpleasant.

"Dr. Walker, there's a..." The girl looked up at me.

"Robin Starling."

"...a Robin Starling here to see you."

"Bring her in."

The girl stood. "If you'll come this way."

As I followed her the half-dozen steps to the open door, the woman whose picture I'd seen on the college's website rose from her desk and came forward with a hand extended. We shook.

"Hi," I said. "I appreciate you taking the time to talk to me."

"Not at all," she said in her trombone voice. "It's what I'm here for."

"I'm investigating the death of Christopher Woodruff, and I'm hoping for some background."

"Are you with the police?" She gestured me to one of her client chairs and walked around her desk.

"I've been hired by Mr. Woodruff's widow. I'm a lawyer."

She frowned. "Representing her on the murder charge?"

"As of right now there is no murder charge. I'm helping her with insurance and other matters."

"People are saying she did it."

"In a situation like this, people are going to say a lot of things."

"Ghastly business." Her trapezius muscles bulged around her thick neck as she gave her head a shake. "So what kind of background do you want?"

"I understand Mr. Woodruff's job title was assistant professor of business. What did he teach specifically?"

"A lot of things. He had an MBA, but was eligible to teach in five different subject areas."

"What does it take to be eligible to teach in a subject area?"

"A master's degree and eighteen graduate hours in the teaching field. He had the M.B.A. Instead of pursuing his doctorate as any sensible person would do, he racked up eighteen graduate hours in economics, finance, accounting, management, and marketing. Probably not the best thing for career advancement, but it made him very useful to us. He could teach pretty much everything we offer."

"What was he teaching this semester? I guess it's still going on."

"Introduction to business, personal finance, micro- and macroeconomics..." She reached for a sheaf of papers stapled at the corner, flipped a few pages, and added, "Also principles of marketing and two sections of accounting, seven courses in all. He was a workhorse."

"Who's covering his classes now?"

"I've taken over the economics courses. The others I've parceled out as best I can."

"Was he a good instructor?"

"Very popular, very good with the kids. I shouldn't call them kids. A school like ours has a good number of nontraditional students, too, some of them older than I am."

"Peyton Shilling?"

She frowned. "The name's familiar. I think she's in one of the economics classes I have now. Macroeconomics."

"When does it meet?"

"Why?"

I tilted my head and aimed for the mildest of shrugs. "Really I'd like his whole schedule if I could get it. It would help me reconstruct the last week of his life."

"Why the interest in Peyton Shilling?"

"It's just a name that's come up. I thought maybe she was a student of his." I wasn't being entirely forthright—okay, I was lying—but I was afraid that too much candor would shut Dr. Walker up as effectively as a fishbone lodged in her throat.

"I wouldn't want anyone contacting students and getting them upset."

"Of course not. But take the morning Chris Woodruff was killed. Did he have an eight o'clock? Did he get in late the night before from teaching class? I need some kind of timeline just to get a sense of context."

She nodded, and her thick, wavy hair remained immobile, as if it were molded plastic. "I understand."

I smiled in what I hoped was a winning way, though I may have just looked sick.

In the end, I got what I came for: A schedule of classes complete with room numbers. Woodruff's next class had been Personal Finance at 4:00, which gave me about an hour to kill if I wanted to look in on it. I wandered through the buildings until I stumbled on the Berrywood Café on the main floor of Burnette Hall. In the middle of the afternoon, only two of the tables were occupied. I wasn't particularly hungry, but I got a cup of coffee and a cookie and went to sit at a table adjacent to one of the tables with students, three females. You'd think that the recent murder of one of their professors would be causing comment, but no such luck. The boyfriend of one of the girls had evidently drunk ouzo the night before until he'd thrown up.

"He was crawling as fast as he could, trying to get to the bathroom, but he didn't quite make it, and he left a trail of vomit over about six feet of carpet."

"Gross," observed another girl.

"Yeah. It took a while to clean up. I kissed him and put him to bed before I went to work on it."

"You kissed him?" A squeal of incredulity.

"I didn't want him to feel bad, did I? I mean, he had enough to deal with."

"I'd have at least made him brush his teeth."

I took another sip of my coffee, but decided I didn't want my cookie. I didn't want to hear any more about vomit either. I put the cookie, still wrapped in plastic, in my purse before moving to a table closer to the other group of students, this one with two guys and two girls leaning over a laptop computer. One of the girls at the first table noticed me moving away from them, and they leaned into the center of the table, whispering and giggling. I was only thirty-one, but I felt like I could have been a contemporary of their grandmothers.

The students at my new table were looking at an Excel spreadsheet, while one of them explained how he had gone about calculating the value of a twenty-year bond after interest rates had risen two percent. It wasn't my field, but it sounded like a personal finance topic, which might mean they would soon be going to the class formerly taught by Chris Woodruff.

Feeling a hunger pang—a faint one, but you can't be too careful—I got out my cookie and unwrapped it. It turned out that the students at my newly adopted table were more interested in the time value of money than in salacious gossip, which was a serious failing, at least from my perspective. I nibbled at my cookie, but after fifteen or twenty minutes of hearing about ordinary annuities and annuities due, I wrapped up what was left of it and put it back in my purse.

What was I hoping to accomplish anyway? The four-o'clock class was about to start, but it wasn't Peyton Shilling's class anyway. If I wanted to learn anything useful, I was going to have to ask questions, and before I did that I was going to have to work out an approach that would encourage students to talk to me rather than close ranks against the outsider.

I stopped halfway to the door. A girl was sitting by herself at a table in the corner. She was holding a tablet computer as if she were reading it, but was looking over the top of it at me.

After a moment's hesitation, I went to her table. "You waiting for class to start?"

"Yes."

"May I?" I indicated a chair.

She shrugged, and I sat. "Personal finance?" I suggested.

"Yes."

"Who's teaching that, now that…you know."

"Now that our instructor has been brutally murdered?"

"Yes," I said. "Now that that."

"Someone named Greg Hardon." She gave a little too much accent to the last syllable.

"You've got to be careful how you pronounce that one," I said.

"I was being very careful."

"Does he hit on girls in the class or something?"

She smiled, shook her head. "Actually, he's a broken down old man, probably seventy or so. It was the middle of the semester, and they were scrounging around for anyone they could get."

When she didn't explain further, I said, "Why the careful pronunciation?"

"I don't know. Dirty minded, I guess. Actually, the name would have fit Mr. Woodruff better. The gods have no sense of humor."

"Greek or Norse?"

"What? Oh, I get it. The gods. You're funny."

"I try. Are you saying Mr. Woodruff hit on women?"

"Maybe. What's your interest?"

I sighed. Sometimes I hated to admit to anyone I was an attorney, but I said, "I'm a lawyer representing the widow. Chances are, she's going to be charged with killing her husband."

"I'd say she had good reason."

"That's not what I want to hear."

"Gives her motive?"

85

I nodded. "On the other hand, I would be interested in the details."

"Prurient interest?"

"Sure. I wouldn't want you to miss class, of course."

"We've got time."

"Meaning you don't know much?"

"Meaning I don't know anything. Just gossip."

"Gossip's good."

"I guess. Have you ever seen Chris Woodruff?"

"Not in the flesh. I've seen a picture."

"He's good looking, isn't he?"

"Sure, if you like that strong-jawed, wavy-haired, clean-featured type." I shrugged. "Okay, he's good looking."

"That's one reason he always had so many people in his classes, so many women anyway. Of course, he was a good teacher, too, one of the best around here. And he was very available outside of class. He kept his office hours, and if you went by to see him, he was always happy to talk to you."

I nodded.

"Except when his door was closed. You'd wait, and eventually the door would open and a student would come out—always female, occasionally a little rumpled looking. That's what they say. I never saw it myself."

"So it wasn't like he fastened on one student," I said.

"I think he usually had a favorite, but you're right. Mr. Woodruff belonged to all women."

"You?"

"Look at me."

"What do you mean? You've got good skin, nice hair, weight in proportion to height…"

She tilted her head as if considering. "Maybe."

"All you need is self-confidence and an interest in making it with a married man."

She smiled. "I guess I'll never know."

"Do you know a woman named Peyton Shilling?"

"That would be the current favorite."

"They say," I said.

"They say. Again, it's just gossip."

"So she's not a friend of yours?"

She shook her head. "She's older than most of us, twenty-six or seven, I think. Maybe even older."

Wow, I thought. Even older than that.

"The word is Mr. Woodruff even moved in with her for a while, but things got messy, and he moved out again. I think she got possessive on him."

"I saw some stuff on Instagram," I said.

The girl smiled. "Me, too. A lot of us, actually. It wasn't like she was discreet or anything. I heard she called his home even when she knew he wasn't there, just to stick it to the wife."

Gossip sure made the rounds. "You make Peyton sound like she's not a very nice person," I said.

"Oh, she's not nice. Drop dead gorgeous, but not nice." She glanced at her phone and stood. "Time's up. I've got to get to class."

The café had cleared out without my noticing.

"I'm Robin Starling, if you ever have anything more you want to tell me. Two bird names, easy to remember."

"I don't think I'm going to tell you my name. Really, I've just been repeating gossip. I wouldn't want to testify or anything."

"They wouldn't let you, if all you know is gossip."

"Good to know."

I got up and walked with her to the door. "Of course, I like gossip," I said. "And I'm always ready to hear more."

She nodded, but turned away from me as we went through the door. I watched her walk to the next building. She was wearing jeans and a pullover, carrying a backpack on one shoulder. Nothing wrong with her looks, but she was pretty ordinary somehow, despite what I had told her. Probably too serious-looking to appeal to the Chris Woodruffs of the world.

I left off speculating and headed for my car. I had a dog waiting for me and maybe time for a run before Paul showed up.

Chapter 5

Or maybe not. When I turned onto my street, Paul's car was parked on the curb in front of my house. I turned onto the side street and into my alley and from there into the garage, and I entered the house through the kitchen. Paul was in my living room watching a rerun of *The Big Bang Theory*.

He pressed mute on the remote. "How was it?"

"Don't you ever work?"

"I was out of town first part of the week. They cut us some slack."

"You were at a two-day conference in D.C. being wined and dined like one of the lords of heaven."

"You want to keep your government officials happy, don't you?"

"Not that happy."

"Oh, you wouldn't like us when we're not happy."

I let it go. "You didn't get Deeks," I said. "Deacon."

"You know why. If I get Deacon, he won't let me in the house. I know he's still a puppy, but he's up to sixty or seventy pounds. He can be a scary guy."

It was true. Deacon loved Paul, but he had taken it into his head that Paul wasn't supposed to be in the house when I was away. I'd tried explaining the situation, but you know how dogs are.

"He's happy over at Dr. McDermott's. They both enjoy the companionship," Paul said.

"Fair enough."

We were crossing the street to Dr. McDermott's when my cell phone rang. It was Carly. I swept my thumb across the screen.

"Hey, Carly."

"The police are here." Her voice was soft, pitched lower than usual.

"What do they want?"

"They're searching your office."

"What? You mean they're presenting you with a search warrant, or they're actually in my office?"

"They're already in your office."

"Who's there specifically? McClane?"

"Is he the fireplug with the flat-top?"

"Yeah, that would be him." Carly, while not as tall as I was, was every bit as tall as McClane, who had the shoulders and barrel-shaped torso of a much taller man. "Can you...never mind. I'll try him on his phone."

I punched off. "Trouble," I said to Paul. We were on the front stoop of Dr. McDermott's house when I found McClane's number in my Contacts list. I punched it just as the door opened and Deacon surged out to jam his nose between my knees. For some reason I wasn't ready for it, and I staggered back a step, Deacon following me, his tail a blur. I scratched his head with my free hand.

"McClane."

"The police are searching her office," Paul said quietly to Dr. McDermott.

Dr. McDermott stepped back, and Paul and Deacon followed him inside.

"What the hell are you doing in my office?" I said to McClane. I had planned to stay out on the porch, but the breeze was turning colder, and I hadn't put back on my jacket for the walk across the street. When I went inside, though, I turned toward the kitchen instead of following the others to the living room.

"Well, good to talk to you, too," McClane said.

"You can't search my office. I've got attorney work-product in there. Searching my office is a violation of attorney-client privilege; it's a violation of my client's Sixth Amendment right to effectiveness of counsel; it's—"

"Don't get your panties in a twist. We're not opening any file folders, and your laptop's not even here. We just want the pistol, which you yourself have admitted you have."

"Had. Past tense. And a subpoena's the appropriate way to handle this, not a search warrant."

"We tried a subpoena, remember? And it got us squat. If you've got a problem with the new tactic, take it up with Aubrey Biggs, not me."

"How long have you been there?"

"Not long."

"It shouldn't take you more than fifteen minutes to satisfy yourselves there's not a gun in my office." I hoped there wasn't a gun in my office.

"We want to be thorough, be sure we've considered every possible hiding place."

I took a few deep breaths.

"If that's everything," McClane said in preparation to punching off.

"Do you have the D.A.'s number on your phone?" I said. "I don't think I've got it."

"I think I can do that much for you. After all, we're such good friends." There may have been a touch of sarcasm there. Once upon a time, he had bought me coffee, and his wife had showed up in my office, and…well, suffice it to say, we weren't especially good friends.

Dr. McDermott, who had come into the kitchen without my noticing, laid a phone book on the table by my elbow. I nodded my thanks.

"Here it is," McClane said. He read it out to me. I didn't have a pen handy, so I closed my eyes and made an effort to remember it, then punched off without saying goodbye and dialed.

Aubrey Biggs, at least according to his secretary, was on another call.

I punched off violently. Deacon was there nuzzling my leg. I put down my phone to rub his ears, but he yelped and pulled away.

"You're expression's as dark as a thundercloud," Dr. McDermott said.

"Sorry. Sorry, Deeks." He was back with his tail wagging, my apology accepted before it was made, and I rubbed the top of his head more gently. "The police are searching my office."

"That's what Paul said. Can they do that?"

"Evidently. I don't have to like it."

"May I offer you a hot beverage?"

My eyes went to Paul, who had gotten Dr. McDermott started on *The Big Bang Theory* a couple of months ago. The offer got a smile out of me, but I shook my head.

"Something stronger, perhaps? I've got Scotch, or we could open a bottle of cabernet."

I stood, and my gaze was caught by the cars in front of my house, one of them a police car. My front door was standing open. "Holy cow!" I brushed past Paul, headed for the front door and moving fast—though not as fast as Deacon, who stayed right with me, even anticipating me so that I had to dance around his wriggling body to keep from tripping over him or stepping on his paws. It allowed Paul to catch up to me, and his hand closed over mine as mine closed on the doorknob.

"You can't take Deacon."

He was right. There was no telling how Deacon would react to unaccompanied strangers inside his house. It could get chaotic, and Deacon might get hurt. "Hold him," I said.

Paul didn't trust to the collar, which Deacon had slipped out of before when highly motivated. Paul knelt and hugged him, one arm around his chest behind his front legs and the other around his chest in front of them. I opened the door and went through it, conscious of Deacon's toenails scrabbling against the tiled floor of Dr. McDermott's foyer. The door closed behind me, and I ran down the sidewalk to the street.

Matt Tarrant met me in the doorway of my house.

"What do you think you're doing?" I said, and he handed me a sheaf of papers. It was another search warrant. They were looking for the M&P Bodyguard or any other handgun that might have been used in the murder of Christopher Woodruff.

"You tell your boss I won't forget this," I said. "I'm going to be out for blood."

"If you mean the chief, he doesn't have anything to do with this. It's all Aubrey, all the time. Besides, if we find what we're looking for, your ass is going to be in jail." He looked at me over the rims of his glasses with his pale, watery eyes.

I started past him into the house, but he stopped me with a hand on my arm.

"I'd like for you to stay out here with me," he said. "Better not to get in the way.

I held up the papers he'd given me. "What we'd like and what we get are often two different things."

"Robin. Don't start something here. There's nothing in it for you."

"If your men are going to trash my house, I'm going to watch them do it."

And I did. There were four uniformed men in the house, and I watched them take out my dishes and glasses from the kitchen cabinets and set them on the counter, go through the stuff in my freezer, poke metal rods down into my canisters of flour and sugar and coffee. In my bedroom, they emptied my drawers and got up on a step-stool to shine a flashlight into the corners of my closet shelf. They took the lids off my toilet tanks. They looked under beds and under sofa cushions, and they lifted out my TV to see if anything was behind it or taped to the back.

Actually, the four of them were spread out through the house, working independently, and I don't know what all they did, but they seemed to make a thorough job of it, checking out not just the house proper, but the front porch, the back patio, the garage, and of course my car. About forty-five minutes into it, Paul showed up, without Deacon, and he found me in the laundry room that separated the kitchen from the garage. I met his gaze and grimaced, and he gestured with his head back in the direction he had come.

I followed him. Matt Tarrant was in the living room, standing with his hips propped against the back of my sofa. He turned his head as we came in.

"If you find anything, it will be because somebody planted it," Paul said. "You can see what they did to the French door." I hadn't yet replaced the broken pane, though I had cleaned up the glass so Deacon wouldn't cut himself and cut a rectangle of cardboard out of a box to tape over the opening.

"You didn't report a break-in," Tarrant said.

"I don't think that's how they got in," I said. "The window was broken from the inside."

"Interesting."

"It would be nice if someone other than me thought so."

"I don't disbelieve you."

"But you don't believe me either."

"I'm suspending judgment."

"Great. See how far that gets you."

Paul was standing with his leg against the end table, his body hunched slightly so that his fingertips touched the surface. I looked at him quizzically, but he didn't meet my gaze. My eyes moved down his arm to the end table where a cell phone leaned against the base of the lamp.

My mouth went dry. It was a cell phone, but not an iPhone. Not mine. And not one I'd ever seen before.

Fortunately, "cell phone" wasn't on the search warrant. Two hours or so of searching failed to turn up a Smith & Wesson Bodyguard or any sort of firearm. The uniforms left, but Matt Tarrant hung back to say, "I think we've misjudged you."

"Well, thank you, but it's a little late for that. I've got this mess to clean up."

"You're even more devious than everybody says you are."

"Maybe I'm just innocent. Has anyone considered that?"

He gave me a weak smile. "Time will tell," he said.

I closed the door behind him, and Paul and I went back to stand over the phone.

"Should we touch it?" he said.

"I think I'd like Rodney to dust it for prints. Not that there are likely to be any."

"Doesn't it make you nervous that someone keeps walking in and out of your house like he owns the place?"

A shiver started between my shoulder blades and worked its way outward. It evidently showed.

"I'll take that for a yes," Paul said.

"You know, I misplaced my keys for a while early in the week. Tuesday. Had to borrow Brooke's car that afternoon and everything."

"Where did you lose them?"

"Carly ran across them in the kitchen later that afternoon. They were on the counter next to the coffee maker."

"Do you remember taking your keys into the kitchen?"

"No. I'm not saying I didn't, but I can't imagine why I'd have been carrying them around. I missed them when I got back from lunch, and Carly had to let me in my office."

"You need to have all your locks rekeyed."

I glanced at the time on my DVR. "It's too late to do it today," I said.

"You know that means I'm staying here again tonight." He held up his hands. "And don't worry about hygiene. I went by my apartment before I came out here, and I've got enough clean underwear to last me a week."

The next day was Friday, and I have to say, I was ready for the week to be over. I gave the cell phone we'd found to Rodney Burns and asked him to check for fingerprints. When he brought it into my office about thirty minutes later, he was carrying it with latex gloves.

I looked up into his face. "Anything?"

He shook his head solemnly. "Nothing, not even smudges."

"Do you think someone wiped it clean?"

"That would be my guess." He placed the phone on the desk and turned it to face me.

"Do you know whose it is?" I asked.

He shook his head. "I didn't even try to turn it on."

"Let's see." I put a thumb on the screen to hold the phone in place and pressed the button on the top edge.

"You do realize your prints are on the phone now," Rodney said as the Samsung logo winked on.

"But now I'll feel no compunctions about wiping them off."

The wallpaper that replaced the Samsung logo was a picture of a very young child who I thought might be Caden Woodruff. I swiped the screen and was invited to enter the passcode.

"Do you recognize the baby?" Rodney asked.

"I don't know. Maybe." I wondered what Caden's birthday was. The easy way to find out—the cheap way, at least—was to call Willow and ask her.

"I think it's Caden Woodruff," I said. "Son of the murdered Christopher. I don't guess you could get me his date of birth, could you?" The screen went dark.

"Probably. You think that's the passcode?"

"Maybe. Could be Willow's birthday or Chris's, or their anniversary—or anything else for that matter. Let's try the boy's birthday first. If that doesn't work, I'll call Willow and ask her if she knows the passcode for her husband's cell."

Rodney nodded gravely, and he left my office. I moved the phone to the edge of my desk, noted my purse on the floor beside me—in my rush to get the phone to Rodney, I'd just slung it against the right pedestal of the desk—and opened the drawer to put it away.

A black semiautomatic stared up at me. I shut the drawer and sat back. A poltergeist was playing games with me. I opened the drawer again, almost expecting to find the drawer empty this time, but the pistol was still there. I leaned over it, staring. It was a Smith & Wesson M & P Bodyguard.

"Robin?"

My insides lurched as I sat bolt upright, slapping the drawer shut. It was Brooke Marshall.

I exhaled tentatively.

"You look like you've seen a ghost."

"Funny you should say that."

She came in and sat down, but I was trying to think and found it difficult to meet her gaze.

"What's wrong? You're scaring me."

"I need a man," I said.

"What? That's sudden. Shall I ask Rodney if he has a few minutes, or can you wait for Paul to get over here?"

"A man's voice," I said. "I need a man to make an anonymous call from the food court out at Regency Square Mall."

"What is it?"

I shook my head. "It's better if you don't know, if nobody does."

"How about the man you need," she said slowly. "Can he know?"

I grabbed my purse by the strap as I stood up. "I'm going to the mall."

Brooke stood, too. "Okay. I'm going with you."

"You've got work."

"As it happens, no appointments all morning."

I focused on her. "Good. You can drive. I'll call Paul on the way, maybe he can meet us." I hesitated a moment, then unzipped my purse, took a pencil off the desk, and bent over the side drawer. Slipping the pencil into the barrel of the gun, I lifted it out of the drawer and into my purse. I zipped the purse shut.

"Is that…," Brooke began.

"Don't talk. Not here."

Brooke bumped into Rodney as she went through the door, and I ran into her back.

"Whoa," Rodney said, retreating. "Excuse me."

"I've got to go," I told Rodney.

"I got that date you asked for. Thanksgiving Day year before last. November 24."

"Thanks."

As we entered the reception area, Carly said brightly, "Hey, girls. Any new surprises this…" She trailed off. "There are, aren't there?"

My mouth twitched. "Aren't there always? Listen, could you do me a favor while I'm gone? Someone's been going in and out of my office like it was his own. Could you have the lock on the door rekeyed?"

"I guess so. Sure. Is anything wrong?"

"Not yet. I'm inches away from catastrophe, but I haven't gone over, not yet."

"She's a bit on edge," Brooke said.

"How do you know it's not Carly going in and out of your office?" Brooke said as we speed-walked down the sidewalk toward our parking garage. "She has a master key."

"It has to be someone with a connection to Chris Woodruff, but you're right. If it's Carly, rekeying the locks won't help."

"Carly could have gotten your keys out of your office while we were at lunch Tuesday, then pretended to find them in the kitchen."

"That would have allowed her to copy the key to my house, too," I conceded. "I can't see Carly as the sinister character you're suggesting, though. You don't know of any connection to the Woodruff family, do you?"

"No."

We concentrated on breathing until we got to the parking garage. "It's an idea, though," I said as we huffed our way up the stairs. "I may have

Rodney…check out the owner of…the Executive Suites…maybe the whole list of tenants."

"That's going to run into…some bucks," Brooke said.

"Yeah, maybe."

We reached the level where we'd parked our cars. "Can we take your car?" I said. "I've got to wheedle Paul."

"Sure."

We went to her CR-V. As she wound down out of the garage, I punched Paul's name on my speed dial, and his face filled the screen.

"Hey, Paul," I said when he answered. "Brooke and I are on our way to Regency Square. Can you meet us for an early lunch?"

"It's ten o'clock."

"It's kind of an emergency. I'll explain it when I see you, but I'm hoping you can leave right now."

"Just a minute." I heard him talking to someone, then he came back. "Can do," he said.

"Fifteen minutes?"

"Better give me thirty."

"Good man."

I punched off, and Brooke said, "So what's the plan?"

"I'm going to dump the gun."

She shot me a glance, opened her mouth to speak, then shut it again. She merged the car onto the Downtown Expressway and accelerated. I waited. Finally, she said, "Isn't that tampering with evidence?"

"I'm not thinking of it that way."

"How would the D.A. think of it?"

"As tampering with evidence. Hear me out, though. Suppose I call the police and tell them I now have the murder weapon, assuming that's what this is. What are they going to think?"

"That you had it all along."

"That I had it all along, and that I got it from my client. It smears me, and it smears Willow Woodruff, probably in a way that's going to be admissible in court. It isn't fair to either of us. And it seems to me that all this gun-shuffling has been orchestrated for just that effect."

Brooke nodded. "Why the rush, though? We went tearing out of the office like our pants were on fire."

"The gun was in my desk because somebody planted it. This somebody has tipped the police before. For all we know, the police are back in my office right now."

Brooke whistled. As she maneuvered into the lane that would put us on I-64, she said, "You could plant the gun on someone yourself. Peyton Shilling is the obvious candidate."

"I thought of that, but that would be just as unfair as what this unknown tipster is doing to me and Willow Woodruff. Peyton's a home wrecker and a nasty piece of work, but I don't have any particular reason to believe that she killed Chris Woodruff."

"Motive," Brooke said. "A woman scorned."

"I'll use that if I need to, believe me, but hanging the murder weapon around her neck is a different proposition altogether. If this is the murder weapon, the police need to have it, but they need to get it in a way that's entirely neutral."

"If it is the murder weapon and it's registered to Willow, the police may arrest her as soon as they get it."

I nodded. "I know. I wish it could be helped."

"So what's Paul for?"

"To call in another anonymous tip."

"Why call it in? Why not just dump the gun and be done with it?"

"That would be a crime," I said. "Chris Woodruff has been murdered, and the police need the murder weapon."

"Isn't what you're doing a crime, too?"

"Maybe. Yes. I can't think of any other way to handle it that's fair."

"Maybe it's like that tree that falls in the woods." She glanced at me. "If there's no one to witness it, is it still a crime?"

I smiled, my eyes on the road as the broken lines on the pavement slipped by us. "Brooke Marshall, you're a philosopher after my own heart."

Regency Square Mall was in sight when I had Brooke turn into the parking lot of a Long John Silver, home of fast-food seafood, most of it fried. There were no other cars in the lot, and there was a dumpster in back of the restaurant, both of which seemed promising. When Brooke stopped the car beside the dumpster, though, I could see across some curbing to two other restaurants and a motel and could see cars going by on both Parham and Eastridge Roads. We were in eyeshot of a lot of people. How many of them might remember a tall blonde get out of a car in an empty parking lot and throw something in a dumpster? My eyes cut toward Brooke, who was less tall...but probably just as striking with her clear, freckleless skin and thick red hair.

"What?" she said. "I don't like it when you look at me that way."

"I'm just wondering which of us would be less noticeable getting out of the car to open the dumpster and toss something in." Paul, I thought, would be less noticeable than either of us. We could drop him off and let him walk half-a-block or so until he found an inconspicuous place to slip the gun out of his pocket and into a dumpster or a trashcan or a bush. Then we could swing around and pick him up.

"If that door on the side of the dumpster was open, we could toss it in without either of us getting out of the car. All we'd have to worry about then is someone remembering the license plate."

"It's not open."

"Well if you're going to nitpick…"

I pointed. "See that station on the other side of Eastridge? Let's go get some gas."

As Brooke drove us over there, I looked around in her car for some trash to wrap the gun in. There wasn't anything. "You're a neat freak, you know it?"

"You say that like neatness is a bad thing."

"Just inconvenient to me personally," I said. "At least at the moment. Never mind. There're paper towel dispensers on the posts."

Brooke stopped at a pump and we got out. As she looked at the pump. I pulled out a couple of blue paper towels.

"You can't actually get gas, you know," I said. "There can't be any record of our being here." I walked back around the car and leaned in to get the handgun out of my purse, using the paper towels both to avoid leaving prints and to hide the gun from any casual observers. As I walked back toward the pump and the trashcan beside it, I wiped my hands on the bundle of paper towels. I dropped the bundle into the trash.

Brooke was already back behind the wheel. I walked back around the car and got in.

"Does it look suspicious that we pulled up and pulled away again without pumping gas?" she asked as I pulled the door shut.

"Probably. Hopefully not suspicious enough that anyone will remember it a couple of hours from now. The main thing is that no one can describe us to the police." In the side mirror I saw a white pickup pull up to the pump we had just vacated. Then Brooke turned onto Eastridge, and we were away clean. I hoped.

Paul beat us to the food court. When we walked in, he was seated at a table, sipping a drink through a straw. He was wearing khakis and a polo shirt with the Federal Reserve Bank of Richmond logo embroidered on the left breast. The time was not yet eleven on a Friday morning. Only half the vendors were open, and only Paul's table and a couple of others were occupied.

"Don't make eye-contact," I murmured to Brooke. "Just walk past him into the mall."

Paul opened his mouth to say something as we neared his table, but he closed it again and picked up his drink for another sip as we walked by. Good boy.

Brooke and I turned the corner and walked down the mall a few storefronts, then sat on a bench in the middle of the mall. After a few minutes, Paul appeared. He sat at another bench that had its back to ours, still not looking at us, and said to no one in particular, "Does someone want to tell me what this is about?"

"I need you to make an anonymous call to the D.A.'s office."

After a few moments' reflection, he said, "I assume you want it made from the pay phone near the food court."

"Yes. I want it tied to the previous tip, and that one came from here."

"You got a phone number?"

"Brooke's looking it up."

Brooke glanced at me, then got out her phone to do it.

"What am I supposed to say?"

I reached for my purse, realized I didn't have what I needed. "Got a pen?" I said.

He had one clipped in the placket of his shirt. He pulled it out and handed it to me over his shoulder.

"Anything to write on?"

He rolled his eyes, then got out his wallet and extracted a receipt folded multiple times. He held that over his shoulder, too, and I took it. I looked around for a hard surface to write on before deciding I'd have to make do with the arm of the bench. Brooke held out her phone, which displayed "Biggs A" over the address of the Commonwealth's Attorney on East Broad Street and a phone number. I copied the phone number onto the back of the receipt, then after a little thought composed the message that would let Aubrey know a semiautomatic pistol was in one of the trash cans at the Valero station near Parham and Eastridge.

I looked at Brooke, who was watching me write. In a low voice, I said, "You don't remember the number of the pump where we dumped the gun, do you?"

She shook her head.

"Well, why make it easy for them?" I made an edit, then handed the note over my shoulder to Paul. For a while he continued to sit, an elbow on the back of his bench, gazing abstractedly down the mall.

"What is it?" I asked.

He exhaled audibly. "Someday you're going to get me into doo-doo so deep you're not going to be able to get me out of it, aren't you?"

"We can hope not."

"That makes me feel a lot better." He sighed again and stood up.

"Don't come back here when you're done," I said. "Meet us at Fuddruckers. My treat."

Chapter 6

When I got to the Ironfronts on Monday morning, I had a new key waiting for me. I said hi to Carly, and as she answered, she slapped a lone key on the counter and slid it toward me.

I picked it up. "Thanks, Carly." I'd had my own locks changed Friday afternoon after the lunch at Fuddruckers. Paul had to get back to work, but Dr. McDermott helped me take off the doorknobs and door levers, five in all, then he had stayed in the house while Deacon and I took them to a locksmith. It would have made sense to leave Deacon with Dr. McDermott, but Deacon had been getting territorial about my house, at least where Paul was concerned, and I didn't want to risk Dr. McDermott getting his pants leg torn off.

The afternoon had become unusually warm for April, and, when I got to the locksmith, I hesitated about leaving Deacon in the car. It would be nice if I'd brought a leash.

"You stay close," I told Deacon.

He came to his feet on the car seat, his tail smacking the dash, and I gave him a crooked smile. "Stay close," I said again and opened the door, holding up a hand to keep him from going out over top of me. "Okay," I said when I was out.

Deacon jumped to my seat and from there to the ground.

"Heel," I said. It wasn't a command I used with him very often. In our neighborhood, the looser "stay close" worked well enough. I was pleasantly surprised that he stayed right beside me as I pulled open the door of the locksmith, and he crowded against my leg as we went through.

"That dog's not on a leash," the guy at the counter said.

"Do you allow dogs in here if they're on a leash?"

"I don't guess we have a policy at all, actually."

"Good," I said. I put my sack of doorknobs on the counter. "I need to get these rekeyed."

He peered into the sack. "You have the keys for them? Save us having to pick the locks."

I got out my keys and took two of them off the ring.

"You want two different keys still, or do you want them all the same?"

"Can you do them all the same?"

"Sure."

"That would be better."

"Hey, Jim," the guy called. "We got work."

An older man, close to fifty, came out of the back. There was a stool on my side of the counter, so I sat on it. Deacon, after giving the place a quick once-over, lay at my feet. It took Jim and the guy at the counter about thirty minutes to change out the locks and cost me just over forty dollars.

"Thanks," I said as I paid. "If I had known it was this cheap and easy, I'd have been getting my locks changed every month or two."

"Feel free to come back," said the guy at the counter.

"That's a good dog you got there," Jim said.

"Thanks. I think so, too."

"Well behaved."

I shrugged and smiled. Though I appreciated the compliment, *well behaved* was a bit hit or miss with Deacon.

When we got back home with the sack of doorknobs, Dr. McDermott had fallen asleep in my recliner. Deacon stopped short when he became aware of him and looked back at me.

"It's okay," I said.

At the sound of my voice, Dr. McDermott started awake and shook his head. "I think I dozed off. Hey, big guy." He dropped a hand over the arm of the chair, and Deacon wiggled over and licked it.

"I was a little worried about how he'd react to finding someone in our house," I said.

"Deacon and I go way back." Almost as far back as Deacon himself did, though that had only been about six months. "And, after all, I let him into my house."

"Maybe he feels a certain reciprocal obligation," I said.

"I wonder how he'd react to finding you in my house," Dr. McDermott said. "We'll have to try it sometime."

I couldn't imagine Deacon challenging me, but it was something to think about. That evening, he and I ran together. On Saturday we took another run and did some yard work together. I called Willow Woodruff in the afternoon just to see how she and Caden were enjoying the warm spring weather.

"Fine. We went to Bryan Park. The azaleas are in bloom, and it's beautiful."

I hadn't ever been to Bryan Park when the azaleas were in bloom. Paul and I needed to go sometime.

"He asked about his daddy," Willow said.

"What did you tell him?"

"That his daddy was in heaven looking down on us." There was a catch in her voice. "I hope it's true. That he's in heaven, I mean."

"Me, too." Both that there was a divine dance to enter into and that, whatever his failings, Chris had reconciled finally with the dancers. "The police haven't bothered you?"

"No. Maybe they're going to leave us alone now."

I was torn between the need to prepare her for what was surely coming and the desire to protect whatever weekend she had left from fear and worry. "I hope so," I said.

That night Deacon and I met Paul at Dogwood Dell's amphitheater for an evening concert given by an R&B group called the Faculty Lounge Lizards. Dogwood Dell was a public park, and I got out my leash for the occasion. There were a lot of people there for the concert, even a few families with kids, and maybe a dozen dogs. I didn't figure all of them wanted to meet Deacon.

On Sunday Paul came over to my place for a long walk.

Though I felt like we'd given Deacon a lot of quality time over the weekend, he was a dog, and for dogs it's never enough. On Monday, he gave me about fifteen minutes with my morning cup of coffee, then used his head to push one of my legs off the couch. When I put it back on the couch; he pushed my foot to the floor again. I gave up and stood to go get my running shoes, and he danced around me. Having a dog made it a lot easier to stay active, I reflected. It made it impossible, really, not to.

I used the new key Carly had given me to unlock my office door, went to my desk, and opened the side drawer to put my purse in it. No gun, just an empty drawer. I let out the breath I hadn't known I was holding.

"This is for you, too," Carly said from the doorway. I could hardly see her behind the spray of roses she was holding.

"You're kidding me."

She set the roses on the desk, and I bent over them to smell the delicate fragrance.

"Paul?" I said. We had had a wonderful weekend, I thought.

"Better read the card."

A small envelope was tucked among the thorny stems. The card inside read, "Roses are red, violets are blue, I get all squishy inside when I think of you." The name under this appalling rhyme was even more appalling: Carter Fox.

"I feel sick," I said.

"I thought you would."

My phone rang, and we both looked at it.

"Maybe that's not him," Carly said.

"Maybe pigs can fly," I said, but I picked up the phone.

"Robin? Robin, is that you?" It was Willow Woodruff, her voice shrill.

"Yes. What's wrong?"

"I'm at the police station at the John Marshall Courthouse. I've been arrested."

I felt a rush of guilt. I had done this to her by making sure the police found her gun. It didn't help to know I couldn't have done anything else without becoming an accessory-after-the-fact.

"Have you been processed, fingerprinted and photographed and everything?" I asked.

"Yes. Robin…What's going to happen to Caden?"

Now I felt a real pang of guilt. I should have made prior arrangements for her son.

"What happened?" I said. "Where is Caden now?"

"The men who came to arrest me, they let me call my neighbor Vicky Roberts, who keeps him sometimes."

"And she came and got him?"

"Yes, she was going to take him to daycare, just like usual, but I don't think she's going to be allowed to pick him up." Her voice dropped, and it sounded like she had her hands cupped around the mouthpiece. "The police were going to call…CPS." She whispered the name just as the Poles might once have whispered *Gestapo*. "Robin, you have to do something. Caden won't do well in foster care. He won't understand it."

I was thinking. I didn't know anything about Child Protective Services. "I've only got a few minutes before I have to head that way for your presentation before the magistrate, but let me see what I can do. In the meantime, don't answer questions. Don't talk to anyone about anything."

"I understand."

"Try not to worry. Maybe we can get a reasonable bail set." When I hung up, I continued to sit with my hand on the receiver. I was surprised to see Carly still there, watching me anxiously.

"Trouble?" she said.

I grimaced, then nodded. "First roses and now a client in jail and a child with no one to care for him."

"Wow," she said.

I called Tom McClane. "Thanks for the heads up," I said when he answered.

"What, I'm supposed to check with you before I do my job?"

"I hope Willow Woodruff has kept her mouth shut," I said. "You are not to question her except in my presence."

"Not that it would do us any good. Pretty much all she's done is carry on about that precious brat of hers."

"She's a mother. Cut her some slack."

"She's a mother who murdered her child's father."

"You haven't established that yet."

"I've established it to my own satisfaction."

"Fortunately the law is going to require a little more." I took a breath. A show of hostility was not going to be profitable at this point. "Did you call CPS?"

"Yes. There's a minor child involved. The mother obviously can't take care of him if she's sitting in a jail cell."

"How about this Vicky Roberts, the neighbor who takes care of him sometimes?"

"Up to CPS."

"Do you know the name of the caseworker?"

"I know the name of the buzz saw I talked to. I guess her official title is caseworker."

I waited.

"Mindy Churchill," he said.

"Do you have a number?"

"I can give you the CPS number I called."

"That will do."

He read it out to me.

"Thanks," I said.

"You owe me."

"Story of my life." I hung up and dialed the number.

It took me awhile to connect with Mindy Churchill. An automated message started to tell me what to dial "1" for, and I pushed "0." There was a pause, and the automated message started over again at "1." I pushed "0" a few more times. Into the resulting silence, I said, "I want to make a complaint."

I don't know what I did that worked—maybe nothing, but the sound on the line changed, and a voice said, "Operator."

"I'm calling for Mindy Churchill."

"Ms. Churchill is on another line. May I connect you to her voicemail?"

"Please."

I left a message that included my cell number. When I hung up, I shoved my purse into my briefcase and headed for the door, stopping short as it swung to behind me. Carter Fox was in the archway, a self-satisfied smirk on his face.

"You like roses, I trust," he said.

"Carter. I'm flattered, but…You know I have a boyfriend."

"A boyfriend is hardly a lifetime commitment."

"But it is a commitment. I really shouldn't accept the roses."

His self-satisfied smile became still broader. "But you will," he said.

"Isn't there anyone else you can give them to?"

"There's no one else I want to give them to."

I sighed. "I can't talk now. I've got to get to the courthouse." My cell phone began to play "It's the End of the World as We Know It," which was my generic ringtone. "Actually, I've got to take this call," I said.

"We'll talk later." He gave me a wink and headed down the hall toward his office.

I put down my briefcase and fished for the keys to my office as I answered the phone. "Robin Starling."

"This is Mindy Churchill. How can I help you?"

I gave her my name again and told her I was a lawyer representing Willow Woodruff. "I'm calling about Caden Woodruff. I think you talked to a police detective named Tom McClane about him earlier this morning."

"Don't remind me."

"I know. It's an occupational hazard for me, too." I reopened my office door, rolled my eyes at the roses that dominated my desk, and put my briefcase on the floor.

"It's not his manner I'm objecting to, you understand. It's that he sent an eighteen-month-old child off with a woman we don't know anything about."

"I understand the mother was okay with it." I dropped into one of the client chairs.

"Is this the mother who's charged with killing Caden's father?"

"Touché, though so far it's just a charge."

"We don't have the luxury of waiting for proof beyond a reasonable doubt when a child's wellbeing is at issue."

"That's the reason for my call, actually," I said. Mindy seemed in the process of mounting her high horse, and I wanted for forestall her. "The mother is almost beside herself with worry about Caden. Is he still at the daycare, or has he already been removed?"

"He's there, but we've been in contact. They're not going to release him except into our custody."

"I guess it gives you a few hours to make arrangements. Is Vicky Roberts a possibility?"

"The woman who took him this morning? We talked to her. She doesn't want him."

"So, what? Are you looking for relatives?"

"Yes. I'll be stopping by the jail to see the mother this afternoon after the ex parte hearing." An ex parte hearing is one held without one of the parties to the controversy—in this case, without the mother.

"Isn't that backwards? Shouldn't you see the mother first to give her notice of the hearing?"

"It's something of an emergency. Caden can't be returned to his home because the only surviving parent is in jail. We've got today."

"The surviving parent might be released on bail. I'm about to head for the courthouse. If we can—"

She cut me off. "She can't retain custody. Given the charge against her, she's going to be able to see Caden only on short, supervised visits, at least until this is settled."

Worse and worse. "Isn't that up to a judge?"

"Yes it is, which is why we're having the hearing this afternoon."

"Where is that going to be, the John Marshall Courthouse? What time?"

There was a silence. "Two o'clock. Juvenile and Domestic Relations Court. District Judge Charles Messer. Do you plan to be there?"

"With the mother, if the sheriff's office will cooperate."

"We're not prepared for an adversary hearing."

"I'm operating on short notice myself. Is there anything I can do for you? Get you contact information for Caden's relatives? I'll bring it to the hearing."

"That would be helpful."

"Is there a form, or…"

"There's always a form. Give me a few minutes, and I'll fax you a copy."

I hung up and sat staring at my roses. When I got up to go see if the fax had come through, I leaned over them to inhale the fragrance. Paul had gotten me roses once. If only he'd been the one to give me these.

Willow was sitting on a bench in a cell in the bowels of the courthouse. A deputy sheriff shut the heavy metal door after me, and Willow looked up, her eyes wide. "Is Caden all right?" she said.

"Still at the daycare where Vicky Roberts left him."

"What happens next? Can you get me out of here in time to pick him up?"

I shook my head. "CPS is involved. They're not going to let you pick him up." I sat next to her on the bench and dug out the form Mindy Churchill had sent me, a Child Protective Resources Form. "We've got a busy day ahead of us. They're going to take you before a magistrate, and we've got a hearing in juvenile court at two."

"What's that?" Willow asked, nodding at the form.

"Something CPS sent me. Do you have any relatives who could take Caden temporarily? Or did Chris?"

"I've got a sister in Texas. We're not close, but she does know about what happened to Chris and all."

I got out a pen and put the sister's name, address, and phone number on the form. "Anyone in Virginia? I don't know much about this, but I think her being out of state is going to slow things down, maybe a lot."

"Chris's parents and brother are in Arlington."

"Okay. Tell me about them."

She gave me their names, told me I was going to have to look up the addresses and phone numbers. "Or you can get the contact information from my cell phone, if the police will give it to you."

"I'd like your house keys, too, if you're willing to let me have them. I need to prowl through Chris's life and learn all I can about every connection he had to everybody. Somebody killed him, and right now I haven't got a clue."

"Peyton Shilling."

"Yes—though right now that's more of a suspicion than a clue." She didn't object, and I added,

119

"Where might I find Chris's passwords to his email and financial accounts and whatnot? Did he keep a list on his computer or on a sheet of paper somewhere?"

She nodded. "I think so. There should be a file on his desktop called *overpass* or *mountain pass*—something with *pass* in it. His passwords are all the same though, *babe-magnet* or some variation of it. The usual one has 3's for the e's and a capital T at the end."

"You put up with a lot, didn't you?"

The corner of her mouth rose. "You don't know the half of it."

"Back to Chris's family. You'd be okay with them taking Caden?"

She nodded. "If somebody's got to. His brother Jared wouldn't do, I don't think. He's about thirty, not married, works for the family business. The parents are all right."

"How old?"

"Early sixties. The dad's sixty-one or –two, the mother's a year or two younger."

"Does Caden know them?"

"Yes. We only see them every couple of months or so, but he talks about them."

"That's good. CPS will have to do a background check, maybe some kind of home study, but we should be able to keep Caden out of foster care." I hoped.

"What happens tonight? You think if they got here, CPS would let Jim and Amy pick him up?"

"Arlington's not that far. I'll give them a call as soon as I get a chance, and we'll give it a try."

"They're not going to be my biggest fans when they find out I've been arrested for killing their son."

"You think they'll believe the charges?"

"Wouldn't you?"

"I don't. That's why I'm here."

She gave me a searching look. "You don't represent guilty clients?"

I moved my head noncommittally. "Not so far anyway. I try to operate under the assumption that when my clients tell me they're innocent, they're telling me the truth. It's stood me in good stead."

Bail was set at six hundred thousand dollars. I knew it would be big, but that was a blow. The deputy sheriff took us back to the cell to wait for Willow's transportation to the Richmond City Jail.

"I need to get Ms. Woodruff's keys and her cell phone out of her personal effects," I told him. "Are those still here?"

"Yeah, they're still here. You'll have to sign for them."

"Sure."

When we were alone in the cell again, I said to Willow, "How interested are you in making bail?"

"I'd love it, of course."

"What can you tell me about your financial assets? The amount of your mortgage, and so on."

"Not much. Chris has some files in his office. I think he handles most things online, though."

"What accounts do you have, do you know?"

"A checking account with Bank of America."

"Okay."

"A brokerage account. Retirement accounts in both his name and mine."

"No savings account?"

She shook her head.

"Any idea what it all adds up to, what your net worth is?"

She shook her head.

"Less than six hundred thousand?"

She snorted.

"Less than two hundred thousand?"

"Probably."

"I might be able to arrange bail through a bail bondsman, but he's going to take at least ten percent."

"Ten percent of what?"

"The six hundred thousand. We'd have to turn over almost everything for collateral, and the ten percent is gone forever. Even if the case is dismissed tomorrow, that's sixty thousand dollars you'll never see again, money that won't be available for you and Caden to live on."

"You talk as if I had a chance of getting out of this," she said.

"Well."

"Any reason for that optimism, or are you just an optimistic person?"

"I don't know. I don't have a reason I can articulate just now. If you're innocent, though, there's something helpful out there. I just need to uncover it."

"So you're just an optimistic person."

"A lot of bad things happen, but they're only a small fraction of all the bad things that could happen."

"That's supposed to encourage me?"

"It means that 95 percent of the things we worry about never come to pass."

"The remaining 5 percent can kill you."

"Well, yes. And of course some of the bad things that happen to you come out of nowhere. You never get a chance to worry about those at all."

"Maybe you're not such an optimist, after all."

I thought about it. "Maybe not," I said. "I still think worry is wasted effort."

I had time to go by the Woodruffs' house before lunch. On the way out there, I called the mobile number Willow had for Chris's mother. Judging just by the timbre of her voice, the woman who answered could have been forty as easily as sixty.

"Hi, Amy. I'm Robin Starling," I told her. "Willow gave me your number."

"My daughter-in-law Willow?"

"Mother-of-your-grandson Willow," I said.

"Okay."

"She was arrested this morning. I'm the lawyer who's representing her."

"So she killed Chris after all."

"I don't think so. At least, I think you should keep an open mind."

"What did you say your name was again?"

I repeated it. "Child Protective Services has an emergency hearing scheduled for two o'clock. They're going to be asking for temporary custody of Caden. Willow is hoping you and your husband can step in to keep him from going into foster care."

"Of course. Things look bad for her then?"

"At the moment. Now that she's in the maws of the criminal justice system, getting her out is going to take time."

"But you will get her out, you think."

"I'm working on it."

"And you really don't think she killed my son."

"No. At least, my working hypothesis is that she's innocent."

"Not a ringing endorsement."

"I haven't known Willow that long. There are things about the case, though, that seem more consistent with her innocence than with her guilt." The appearing and disappearing murder weapon, for instance.

"Okay. I'll accept that for now. What can we do to help?"

"Can you be at the hearing at two o'clock?"

"I'm afraid we can't. We're in Philadelphia at a trade association convention."

"What is your business exactly?" I asked.

"We make school furniture."

"There's a trade association for that?"

"There's a trade association for everything. Ours is the Education Market Association, EdMarket for short. We can get to Richmond by this evening, but we're going to miss the hearing. Where is Caden now?"

"His usual daycare. He was home when the police arrested his mother, but so far his life is still following its familiar pattern."

I was in Chris Woodruff's home office before eleven. He had an all-in-one printer that also served as a scanner, a copier, and a fax machine, so I took advantage of it to fax the Child Protective Resources Form back to the number it had come from, ATTN: MINDY CHURCHILL printed at the top in block letters. If she needed to run background checks on Willow's sister or Chris's parents, I wanted her to have time to do it before the two-o'clock hearing. I tried to get Mindy on the phone to tell her I had sent the fax, but all I got was voicemail. I left a message and turned my attention to Chris's computer.

The computer was password protected, and it took me a few minutes to get into it. The password that got me logged on turned out to be *babemagnet*, no threes, no capital T at the end. There was a file on his desktop called *overpass*. I clicked on it and found two columns of web addresses grouped with, for the most part, variations of the word *babemagnet*. After that it took less than twenty minutes to get a good idea of the Woodruffs' financial situation. They had just under four thousand dollars in a checking account, two retirement accounts with about a hundred-forty thousand between them, a mortgage balance of 219,000 dollars. I looked up the address on the Zillow website for a rough appraisal of their home. It was 265,000 dollars, which gave them a home equity of maybe forty-six thousand.

The bottom line was that Willow didn't have the resources to make bail herself. She might be able to afford a bail bondsman, who might only charge the minimum ten percent on a bail in six figures, but a sixty-thousand-dollar fee would leave her and Caden destitute, at least until the insurance came in. Better for her to wait it out in jail and let her in-laws take care of Caden. Of course, I wasn't Caden's mother. It would have to be Willow's call.

There was a two-drawer filing cabinet in a corner of the room. I looked at my watch. I still had time. I scooted the office chair to the file cabinet and pulled out the top drawer. It contained just what I was looking for: the Woodruffs' financial records.

Fortunately, Chris had been organized to a fault. There was a folder of bank statements he had printed off the web, a folder of brokerage statements, a folder for each of their retirement accounts, a folder that contained forms related to their health insurance, and a house folder that had the deed, the deed of trust, and a collection of closing documents. There was a life-insurance folder, too, but it was empty. Probably the policies Willow had brought me had come from there. Though I knew I could access most or all of the accounts online, I stacked the folders to take with me, including a few that were harder to identify.

The bottom drawer had folders related to various courses Chris was teaching. Nothing of any value now that he was dead. Unless…No, there were no class roster and no grade sheets, graded work, or anything else that might indicate which courses of his Peyton Shilling had taken or how she had done in those courses.

It was a quarter to twelve. I hustled the files out to my car and headed back downtown. My phone rang just as I was turning onto Cary Street. It was Paul.

"Hey, Paul," I said as I answered.

"I thought we were going to go to lunch," he said.

Were we? "Sorry, I got tied up. I'm on my way now, though. Can you wait?"

"That depends. Would it be okay with you if I got Carly to let me wait in your office?"

"Sure. That would be fine."

"Good. Then who's Carter Fox?"

"Who?" Paul was already in my office, I realized. He was sitting at my desk, looking at the vase with its dozen red roses. I passed my parking garage, thinking maybe I could find a spot on Main Street more or less in front of my building.

"The man who sent you roses," Paul said. "Have you forgotten them already?"

"I'm trying."

"So who is he?"

"You know. That lawyer there in the Suites, the one Brooke and I got stuck having lunch with last week. I told you about him. He's no one to worry about."

"Why would a man who's no one to worry about be sending you flowers?"

"Soft in the head? I don't know. I certainly haven't done anything to encourage him."

"Okay."

"Okay?" I spotted a spot on the curb at a parking meter and angled into it.

"He's sure not a poet, is he?" Paul ventured.

"He tries."

"Tries? 'I get all squishy inside when I think of you'? You've got to be kidding."

Obviously, the roses still rankled. "Have you ever written me poetry?" I asked.

"I didn't know you liked it. 'Robin, you're my everything. When I'm with you, I want to sing. Wide my arms I want to fling, to dress you in jewels and lots of bling. My heart begins to go ding-ding...'"

"I don't think *all* the lines have to rhyme. You might try rhyming couplets," I said.

"Maybe I can get a former English major to tutor me." He came through the glass doors of the Ironfronts, saw me getting out of my car, and put up his phone. "There you are."

"Maybe you could help me carry some files up." I walked around to the passenger side of my car. "Do you have time?" He voiced no objection, so I handed him the stack.

As we were riding up in the elevator, I said, "I should have let you keep going, see how many words you can think of that rhyme with ding-a-ling."

"I was just getting started. There are all the gerunds: loving, caring, pining…and of course wing, sting, ca-ching, ring…" He shifted the files he was carrying.

"Ring is an interesting one," I said as the doors began to open on the second floor. "You don't want to get married, do you?"

Brooke and Mike were standing just outside the elevator. Brooke's eyes went wide.

"Wow," Paul said. "Just like that."

"Not to me," I said. "CPS would probably object because I'm representing the mother. You could marry Brooke here."

"What mother?"

"What about me?" Mike said.

"That's right. He could marry you," I said.

"Representing what mother?" Paul said again.

"Willow Woodruff has been charged with murdering her husband. A custody hearing for her son Caden is at two o'clock this afternoon. I'm looking for alternatives to the court turning him over to CPS."

"And you can't take him?" Brooke asked.

"I don't think so. Conflict of interest. Since I represent the mother, I might put her interests over Caden's."

Mike said, "So you're saying it would be convenient for you personally if Brooke and I got married by two o'clock."

I smiled at him. "Would you?"

"Always ready to take one for the team."

Brooke shot him a look, and he pulled her against him.

"Oh, come on," he said. "You know I'm kidding."

She pushed away, and he let his hands drop. "We got along better before we were engaged," Mike told Paul and me. "Too much pressure."

"Mike," Brooke said warningly.

He gave her a wink.

"I didn't think being married made any difference in foster care anymore," Brooke said. "Does it?"

"Don't know," I said. "I'm new to this. Let's go to lunch."

"Can I put these files down first?" Paul asked. "It's not that they're heavy, but I'd feel awkward wagging them along to the James Center."

By way of explanation, Mike said, "Brooke and I were heading that way, thought we'd split a sandwich and have some mulligatawny soup at the Market."

"Mulligatawny soup sounds good," I said.

"And we can talk about your roses on the way. Interesting to learn you've got another boyfriend on the string."

Chapter 7

At two o'clock I was sitting with Willow Woodruff in Juvenile and Domestic Relations Court waiting for the judge—waiting for Mindy Churchill or someone else from CPS, too, for that matter. Except for Willow and me and the deputy sheriff leaning against the side wall, the courtroom was empty.

"What time is it?" Willow asked me. "Are you sure we're in the right place?"

"According to the district court clerk, we are."

"Maybe you should check."

"Let's give it a minute. Someone will show up."

At 2:08 by my cell phone, someone did, a thin, fiftyish woman with wild brown hair who came in with a mass of manila folders clutched against her chest. She pushed through the bar and dumped them on the table across from the one where Willow and I sat, then pushed an errant strand of hair out of her face, trying ineffectually to catch it behind her ear.

"Robin Starling?"

"Mindy Churchill?" I said, standing.

"Yes. I was hoping to be here with one of our attorneys, but everyone's booked."

I gave her a faint smile. "I'm sure this isn't your first rodeo."

"No, but things usually go badly when the other side is represented by a lawyer and we don't have one of our own."

"We can hope," I said.

She gave me a dark look. "You should keep in mind that the well-being of a child is involved," she said.

"It's very much in the front of my mind, along with the thought that bureaucratic solutions aren't always the best. May I introduce you to the child's mother?" I stepped to one side to give them an unobstructed view of each other. "Mindy Churchill, Willow Woodruff."

Willow nodded. Mindy pushed again at the uncooperative strand of hair that had fallen back into her face. "Pleased to meet you, Ms. Woodruff," Mindy said. "It's nothing personal, you understand. We just see so many of these."

Willow nodded.

The bailiff came in and took his place at the corner of the bench. "Oyez, oyez, the Thirteenth Judicial District Court of Virginia is now in session, the Honorable Charles Messer presiding."

A heavyset man in black robes came in and took a seat.

"Be seated." The Honorable Charles Messer was young for a district judge, not much older than I was. He smiled at me, more warmly than I'm used to from judges. Of course, this was the first time I'd appeared before him, so there was still plenty of opportunity for me to alienate him.

"Well, well," Judge Messer said, still smiling at me.

I returned his smile perfunctorily, more unsettled by his obvious friendliness than I would have been by open animosity.

"Well," he said more abruptly, and picked up a file. "We're here in the matter of Caden Woodruff, a minor child."

Mindy and I both stood. "Yes, your honor," we said, almost in unison.

"Representing Social Services is Mindy Churchill. I don't believe I know you, Ms. Churchill."

"I'm not an attorney. This is an emergency hearing regarding custody, and we were expecting it to be ex parte."

"Very well. Representing the parent is…"

"Robin Starling," I said, and he nodded, smiling.

"Robin Starling."

It was like he'd seen me naked. I was starting to get seriously freaked out.

The judge cleared his throat, broke eye contact. "Very well. Ms. Churchill, do you have an opening statement?"

"I do, your honor. The only surviving parent in this case, Willow Woodruff, was arrested this morning on the charge of murdering her husband, who was also the father of Caden Woodruff, the minor child at issue in this case. Before calling Social Services, the Richmond police released Caden into the custody of one Vicky Roberts, evidently a neighbor of the accused. This Vicky Roberts took the child to Stonypoint KinderCare, his usual day care." Mindy consulted her notes, then continued her statement, not telling us anything I didn't already know. What it came down to is that Caden Woodruff had no place to go pending further investigation, and Social Services wanted temporary custody.

When she was done, the judge nodded at me. "Ms. Starling."

"Your honor, Ms. Churchill hasn't mentioned the Child Protective Resources Form that the mother and I filled out and faxed to her this morning. May I?" When he nodded, I took one copy to the bench and another to Mindy Churchill.

She took it, pushing her hair out of her face to glance at it. "We haven't had time yet to follow up on this, your honor," she said.

"I believe Ms. Starling is making her statement, Ms. Churchill."

Her mouth shriveled up like a prune.

"Thank you, your honor," I said. "As you can see, Caden's mother Willow has a sister in Texas."

"Yes, I see that. Wendy Robinson."

"And her deceased husband has parents in Arlington. Though I understand it takes time to deal with all the bureaucratic issues involved with placing a child out of state, the parents present no such difficulties. They are in fact on their way to Richmond now to take custody of Caden. I expect them to arrive sometime this evening."

"Ms. Churchill?"

"We haven't had the opportunity to do background checks, much less a home study. We don't even have the proper signatures that will allow us to get started. We need time, and we ask for temporary custody to give us that time."

The judge looked at me, and I glanced down at Willow, whose eyes were on me, her face wearing an anxious, puppy-dog expression.

"Your honor, the law requires CPS to make reasonable efforts to avoid the need of the child's removal from the home. I don't think they've done that here."

"Your honor, the child's mother has been arrested for murder. Of course the child has to be removed from the home."

"Caden's mother Willow Woodruff asks the court for me to be given temporary custody of her son Caden," I said. "Just until the bureaucratic details can be worked out and the child's grandparents can take custody."

The judge frowned.

Mindy Churchill said, "Your honor, that's ridiculous. There's an obvious conflict of interest here. We need someone who will look first to the child's interest, not someone who is representing the mother."

"Is it true?" the judge asked Willow. "You would like Ms. Starling to take custody of your son until your parents-in-law can be vetted by Social Services?"

She nodded. "Yes, sir."

Judges were *your honor* in the courtroom, but he let the *sir* go. "Ms. Churchill?"

"We very much object to such a disposition because of the very obvious conflict of interest. If the mother were to be released on bail, this would put her right back in contact with her son. You must consider that she has been charged with murdering her child's father."

"Bail has been set at six hundred thousand dollars," I said. "There's no immediate prospect of Ms. Woodruff being able to make it."

"Ms. Starling herself has not been vetted by Social Services," Mindy said.

"Ms. Starling is a licensed attorney and an officer of the court," Judge Messer told her.

"At the very least we need time to do a background check on the grandparents, and before we can do that, we need the grandparents to sign a consent form and to make a written request for custody of the child. It will take too long to leave a child in the hands of the mother's lawyer. You can't award her custody even temporarily. You just can't."

The judge smiled. He was the judge, and this was his courtroom. There was very little he couldn't do.

"I will happily release the child to his grandparents as soon as they arrive," I said.

"That would be most inappropriate," Mindy objected. "Social Services would have to be involved in the transfer."

"Then I suggest you arrange to be involved." The judge picked up his gavel and let it fall. "Temporary custody is awarded to Robin Starling, pending approval of…" He looked at the document I'd given him. "…James and Amy Woodruff as temporary conservators. The court clerk will fill out the order for you."

Instead of leaving the bench, the judge continued to sit there watching us. I went to Mindy Churchill's table and held out my hand, but she only glared at me. "This isn't right," she said.

"I'll give you my address," I said. "You can meet me and the grandparents there this evening to get whatever forms you need filled out."

She didn't say anything, so I leaned over to write my address on one of her folders, then went back to my table.

"Thank you," Willow said, and I gave her a smile.

"All part of the service."

The deputy sheriff led her out. Mindy Churchill gathered her folders and pushed through the rail with them. She took short, quick steps, and her narrow back was rigid. Judge Messer was still on the bench.

"Robin Starling," he said. "You don't remember me, do you? Chuck Messer, Virginia Law Section F. Boy, I remember you."

"Chuck!" I said jovially, trying hard to place him. "Good grief, I don't know why I didn't recognize you. It's hard to think of one of my classmates as a judge, I guess."

"Well, I have gained fifty pounds," he said modestly.

"That's right. You were a beanpole, weren't you?"

"You remember that party when we hooked arms back-to-back, and you bent forward far enough to carry me around, and people fed me chips and cheese cubes and things?"

I placed him then. "You were hilarious," I said. "You kept your knees pulled to your chest and had your head twisted around to get the end of your thumb in your mouth. You were like a baby in a papoose."

He beamed at me, clearly pleased I had remembered him. "It's possible I'd had a little too much to drink," he said.

"I'll say. I guess I'm lucky you didn't throw up on me, getting bounced around like that."

"And don't forget softball. They usually put me in the outfield, but I remember that nothing got by you at shortstop. You were a runner, too. Didn't you win the Race Judicata one year?"

"Two years. A stringy little One-L beat me the third year." I had also run in the Race Ipsa Loquitur all three years, but had never placed better than third. No explanation for the difference except that maybe I ran better in the spring than in the fall, or everyone else ran worse.

"It's been a long time, hasn't it?" Judge Messer said.

We shot the bull for another fifteen minutes or so before people began to file in for the next hearing. "We'll have to get together sometime," he said. "Have lunch or something."

"I'd like that."

I left the courtroom thinking that he hadn't mentioned whether he was married. I hoped the answer was yes and happily, though he hadn't been wearing a ring.

I headed home early, going by the Woodruff house to get the car seat out of Willow's car. When I got to my street, I parked my Beetle in front of Dr. McDermott's house. He answered the door, and, as Deacon boiled out around my legs, he looked past me at my car, a puzzled expression on his face.

"I'm not here for long," I said. "Just long enough to pick up Deacon." I bent over to pat him just as he surged upward to meet me, and his nose hit me in the mouth. "Mmmf," I said, jerking backwards.

"Where are you taking him?"

"To pick up a toddler who's met me only once. I thought Deacon might help me break the ice. You don't think the combination's going to be too overpowering, do you?"

"When you want to be just overpowering enough?"

I had a sudden vision of Caden Woodruff screaming his head off all the way home while Deacon bounded back and forth between the front seat and the back and I weaved back and forth across the road as I tried to control him. "Good point. Maybe I ought to leave Deacon after all. He's got the size of a full-grown dog, and he's still as boisterous as a puppy."

"Maybe you ought to take an old man with you. I'm pretty calm."

Deacon had charged out onto the lawn and was urinating copiously.

"That would be good. Help me control him."

Deacon took the steps in two bounds and jammed his nose between my thighs. I scratched his head.

"Let me get a jacket," Dr. McDermott said. "I'm not as warm-blooded as you spring chickens."

"If you're sure you don't mind."

I left Deacon with Dr. McDermott in the car when I went in to get Caden. There was a girl at the reception desk—a young woman, actually, twenty-something, though she might have been as much as a decade younger than I was.

"Can I help you?" She spoke loudly so as to be heard over all the young voices clamoring somewhere behind her.

"My name is Robin Starling. I'm here to pick up Caden Woodruff."

"Are you with CPS?"

I laid the court order on the counter and turned it toward her. After studying it a minute, she said, "Just a minute," and disappeared back into the building. The sound of children grew louder, then diminished. She came back not with Caden, but with another woman, this one at least a decade my senior. The woman glanced at me, then picked up the court order the young woman had left on the counter. While she read it, a dark-haired man in slacks and a dress shirt came in and, after the young woman fetched a young girl for him, left again with her on his hip, the girl using her hands to turn his head toward her as she started to tell him about her day.

"You're Robin Starling?" the middle-aged woman asked me.

"Yes, I am," I smiled encouragingly as I unslung my purse to get my driver's license.

"I've seen things like this before—parents splitting up, fighting over their child, one or both of them brandishing legal documents. Sometimes CPS is a part of it, but not usually." She looked up from the document and studied me through narrowed eyes. I gave her another smile, but seemed to be running up against the law of diminishing returns. Certainly, it failed to thaw her appreciably.

"I'm going to call CPS."

"Ask for Mindy Churchill. I'll give you ten minutes to get hold of her, then I'll call the police."

She froze with her hand on the phone. "What have the police got to do with this?"

"Nothing yet. But I have a court order granting me temporary custody of Caden Woodruff, and you do not. Withholding him is probably a crime of some sort, though right now I'll just be calling them for help in enforcing the court's order."

She squinted her eyes at me again. "You a lawyer?"

Though my friendly smiles hadn't done much good so far, I gave her my most winning one, tilting my head in a coquettish fashion.

She stepped away from the counter as if I were a cobra that had just flared its hood. "Get him," she said, jerking her head at the young woman.

"Sorry," I said when the young woman had disappeared back into the building again. "It's been a long day. I didn't mean to take it out on you."

The woman nodded, but didn't say anything. The young woman came out leading Caden by the hand.

I took a breath and bent over, bracing my hands on my knees. "Hi, Caden. Remember me? I'm a friend of your mommy's."

He looked up at me with wide brown eyes. "I seen you at my house."

"Yes," I said. "I was at your house."

"What your name is?"

"Robin."

"Wobin," he said. He took his hand from the young woman's and patted his chest. "Caden," he said, then held up a hand with his index and his little finger extended. "Two birthdays."

"Well, hello, Caden with two birthdays." I held out a hand, and he took it. "Do you like dogs?"

He nodded up at me. "Dogs is nice."

"You forgot your papers," the woman said behind me.

140

"That's your copy," I said.

Dr. McDermott was on the far side of the parking lot with Deacon. When they saw us come out, they started toward us, Deacon pulling at his leash until Dr. McDermott gave it a jerk and told him to heel. I was impressed with the way Deacon fell back with his gaze on Dr. McDermott. I mostly walked Deacon without a leash, and, while I maintained a loose control, I could tell Dr. McDermott had done a lot of work with him on-leash.

I stopped with Caden at my VW Beetle. "This is my car," I told him. "I've got your car seat in the back."

He nodded. He hadn't yet seen Dr. McDermott and Deacon, or at least hadn't connected them to us.

"A couple of friends are going to ride with us, an old man and a dog. You like dogs. Right?"

He rolled his gaze up to meet mine, looking uncertain. I opened the car door on the driver's side and pushed the seat forward. "See? There's your car seat. You remember it, don't you?" When he nodded assent, I said, "If you had a choice, who would you want to sit next to you, the old man or the dog?"

Dr. McDermott and Deacon came around the front of the car, and Caden's eyes grew wide. "Doggie," he said.

"This is my dog Deacon. Do you think you'd like him to ride next to you?"

Caden looked back up at me. "Where is Mommy?"

I felt a stab of pain, but kept my expression neutral. "She's not home right now," I said.

"Is she at wuk?"

141

"No, she had to go on a trip. She wanted to take you, of course, but they wouldn't let her. That's why she asked me to pick you up. It won't be for long. Your grandparents are coming to take care of you until she gets back."

He looked unenlightened.

"Your grandparents? Grampy and, ah, Mimi?"

He evidently didn't call them Grampy and Mimi.

"Grandpa and Grandma? Papaw and Gammy?"

"Gammy? P-paw?"

"Yes. Gammy and P-paw. I have a very important question to ask you now. Do you like to be licked?"

"Wike to be wicked!"

"Yes. See the dog there? If he sits in the backseat with you, he's going to get in your face and lick you. Only a few times, and then he'll sit and look out the window. If you don't like that, I can put Deacon in the front seat, and the old man can sit next to you. He doesn't lick."

"I really don't," Dr. McDermott said, smiling. "I'm friendly, but I don't lick."

Caden looked back and forth between him and Deacon. "Doggie," he said finally.

"Okay." I picked up Caden and put him in his seat and buckled him into it. Then I took the leash from Dr. McDermott and walked Deacon around the car. I opened the door on the passenger side and pushed the seat forward. Caden's eyes were wide.

"I don't fink I wike to be wicked."

"He licks me, too," I said. "They're kisses."

"Kissies?"

"Yes, kissies." I squatted beside Deacon and got one on the mouth. "See?"

He nodded solemnly.

I took a breath and gave Deacon some slack. "Hop in," I said. He hopped and I grabbed the leash close to the collar.

"Deacon," I said. "This is Caden. Caden, this is Deacon."

Deacon's nose was strained toward him, his nostrils flaring. He seemed very big in the confined space. "I'm going to let him go now," I said. "He's going to stick his nose in your face, and I think he's going to lick you. Can you be very brave?"

"I fink so." But his voice was trembling.

"Easy, Deeks," I said. "Easy." I gave him some slack, and he stuck his nose in Caden's face as I'd predicted, touching noses, sniffing one of Caden's eyes and then his ear, finally giving him a lick that covered chin to forehead. Caden giggled, and I relaxed. Deacon turned back toward me, and his tail flapped against Caden's car seat.

"He's funny doggie," Caden said.

I stepped back.

"He is a funny doggie, isn't he?" Dr. McDermott said. He pushed the seatback backwards until it locked into place and got in. "Deacon and I are good friends."

I adjusted my rearview mirror so as to keep an eye on Caden and Deacon as we drove. I trusted Deacon, but he wasn't used to small children, and Caden didn't seem to be used to dogs. What I saw was reassuring: Caden watched Deacon with round eyes; Deacon looked out the window. When I got on the Chippenham Parkway and looked again, Caden's hand was stretching slowly toward Deacon. Dr. McDermott had his head turned to watch and was smiling.

Caden touched his hand against Deacon's side and, when Deacon didn't react, exhaled slowly. Then he began to open and close his small hand, giving Deacon a scratch with his fingertips. Deacon turned his head, stretched his neck to give Caden's face a quick lick, then went back to watching the road. Caden giggled.

When we got back to my house, a lime-green Smart car was parked on the street. I pulled up behind it and stopped. Mindy Churchill and I got out. "Hi, Mindy." I pushed my seat up to get Caden, and Deacon jumped to the floor and then past me. He trotted toward Mindy to check her out, trailing his leash, the whole back-half of his body wagging.

Mindy, for her part, backed against her car, holding her hands up under her chin as if she were afraid of getting them bitten off. Deacon gave her dress a lick, then bent his head to sniff at her shoes. Dr. McDermott got out on the passenger side, and Mindy eyed him distrustfully.

"Are you the grandfather?" she said.

"I'm a grandfather, but I think there's more than one of us."

If Mindy had a sense of humor, she didn't show it. "I meant are you Caden's grandfather."

"I am not."

Her gaze turned to me, and I shrugged and reached into the car to get Caden. Deacon moved around Mindy snuffling at her, trying to get behind her but unable to because she was still backed against the car. "You had this large dog in the backseat with the child?" she said.

"And I had an old man in the front seat with me. Don't worry. Neither one of us got pawed."

She didn't smile, but I'll go ahead and concede that my comeback wasn't particularly funny. I set Caden on the ground. Seeing Mindy, he backed against me. I scratched his head, less vigorously than I might scratch Deacon's. "You can see he's fine," I said.

Caden pointed at Deacon. "Doggie," he said. He held out his hand, flapping his fingers against his palm in a summoning gesture. "Heah, doggie."

Deacon turned and looked at him inquiringly, then trotted toward him. Mindy gave an audible intake of breath as Deacon gave his face a lick, then pushed the top of his head against Caden's chest.

"He wants you to scratch his neck," I said.

Caden obliged, working his fingers into the short fur.

"Do you want to wait inside?" I asked Mindy. "I can offer you a hot beverage."

Again, no smile. Probably she wasn't a fan of *The Big Bang Theory*. A pickup turned onto Beechnut, but none of us paid any attention to it until it drew up beside us. The window slid down, and a pleasant-faced woman with gray hair and high cheekbones said, "Which one of you is Robin Starling?"

I raised my hand.

"And there's little Caden. Jim, park the truck."

Jim pulled to the curb ahead of us and got out. He was tall and lean and had a full head of silver hair. Caleb ran to him. "P-paw!" He threw his arms around his p-paw's thighs and embraced him. P-paw scooped him up and handed him to his wife, who had come around the back of the pickup.

145

"Here's Gammy," he said in the cadence of a *Tonight Show* host.

Gammy hugged Caleb fiercely, and Deacon jumped up to put his paws on P-paw's chest.

"Deacon!"

Mindy said to me, "You realize your court order doesn't allow you to transfer Caden to his grandparents until we've run a background check."

P-paw was rubbing Deacon's ears. "Been a long time since I've had a dog," he said.

"How long is that going to take?" I asked Mindy. "Can you get it done tonight?"

"No, I cannot. I can interview them tonight."

"Fair enough. Let's go inside. Deacon!" He dropped to all fours. "Let's go in."

Deacon trotted up the sidewalk and, when he got to the step-up to the front porch, turned to look back at us. P-paw said, "You've got that boy trained."

"I thought I had him trained not to jump."

Dr. McDermott caught my eye, jerked his head toward his house across the street. I held up a hand before he could move off. "Has anybody eaten? Why don't I get you all inside, then I'll go get a sack of burgers. Does that sound good?"

Mindy shook her head. "Nothing for me, thanks."

"Grilled chicken sandwich? Or do you not eat meat at all?"

"I've eaten. I'm not a vegetarian."

"Hot beverage for you," I said. "Dr. McDermott, will you go with me, help me make sure Deacon doesn't put on the sack of burgers like a feedbag before I get it home?"

"Of course."

146

I got them inside and distributed water bottles in lieu of the promised hot beverage, which would have taken longer. I got Caden's attention away from his P-paw for a moment and squatted in front of him. "Caden, do you eat hamburgers? Would you like a hamburger?"

"Bugga," he said. He ran in a circle waving his arms. "Bugga, bugga!"

"Okay," I said, standing. "Bugga it is. Nothing on it but a lot of catsup."

Dr. McDermott, Deacon, and I went out to the car. I held the seat forward, and Deacon jumped into the back as Dr. McDermott was getting into the shotgun seat on the other side. Paul Soldano turned onto the street, and I waited for him.

He drove up beside me. "What's up?" he said as his window opened.

"Got loads of company. Going on a burger run. If you want to come, you can ride in back with Deacon."

He craned his neck to look past me into the back seat. "Do I have to ride in the car seat, or can we put it in the trunk?"

"There's room in the trunk."

So it was a crazy evening. We had burgers, even Deacon, who ate his burger—plain, just meat and bread—on the way home and rode the rest of the way with his nose pressed against one of the sacks with the remaining burgers. Mindy did her interview, which included getting the names of some of Jim and Amy's neighbors she could talk to. I offered to let P-paw and Gammy stay in my spare bedroom for the night, and they accepted. After he ate his hamburger, Dr. McDermott walked back across the street to his home, and Mindy Churchill left about thirty minutes after that. Paul stayed later, keeping me and Deacon company on the back patio while P-paw and Gammy got their grandson to bed.

"So what happens now?" Paul said.

"Tomorrow sometime, with any luck, Jim and Amy Woodruff will get temporary custody of Caden and will head back to Arlington with him. I'll be free to focus on the case against Willow."

"How's that going?"

"Not well."

"Meaning…"

"Meaning I don't know of anything yet that might help her. The arraignment's tomorrow afternoon. I'm going to press for an early preliminary, next week if I can get it."

"Is that smart, given what you've got?"

"It'll give me a look at the prosecution's case, maybe give me something to work on. Right now, I've got nothing."

"Whatever came of Chris Woodruff's phone? Did you get anything off it?"

"No. There was just enough there to make it obvious the phone was his and that it had been wiped clean. I think whoever sent it was just trying to give the police one more reason to charge me as an accessory."

"The police never found out you had it."

"No, I was lucky there."

"Of course, they still think you were playing who's-got-the-button with the murder weapon."

"There's no hope for that."

"Button, button, who's got the button: Did that just start with *Dexter's Laboratory*, or was it around before that?"

"The cartoon? It goes all the way back to *Little Men*, at least."

"Louisa May Alcott? Actually, I had heard of button-button before *Dexter's Laboratory*. I think Tweedle Dee and Tweedle Dum said something about it in *Alice in Wonderland*."

I frowned.

"The Disney version, anyway," Paul said.

"Does everything you know about popular culture come from a cartoon?"

"Pretty much."

Chapter 8

Aubrey Biggs was at the arraignment the next afternoon. He was calm and deliberate, not at all like his usual volatile self. Judge Cheatham asked if I wanted him to read the indictment aloud, and I said I did. I had a copy, but I thought it was always a good idea to drive home to the defendant what we were up against. And the point got driven. The whole time the judge was reading, Willow was looking not at him, but at me, her expression anxious, her eyes pleading. It occurred to me that I was what was standing between her and disaster, and I have to say I didn't envy her.

"How do you plead?" the judge asked Willow.

She wet her lips, and I nodded at her encouragingly.

"Not guilty," she said, almost inaudibly.

He told her she had the right to remain silent, then asked her if there was anything she wanted to say. She shook her head.

"Bail in this case has been set at six hundred thousand dollars?" the judge asked.

Biggs: "Yes, your honor."

"Is that adequate, do you think?"

"We think it is, your honor."

"Is it too much?" Judge Cheatham asked me.

"It's several times her net worth. She can't raise it, and if she uses a bail bondsman it's going to cost her everything she has. In the meantime, she's separated from her two-year-old son."

Judge Cheatham tapped his pencil. "She is charged with first-degree murder," he said to me.

"It's a serious crime, but she hasn't been convicted of it yet. The court's concern is making sure she appears for trial. A quarter-million dollars would be enough to do that."

Cheatham looked at Biggs.

"A quarter-million isn't nearly enough. Her life is on the line." It was a restrained response from Biggs. Really, I felt a lot more comfortable when it seemed like his head was about to explode.

"We'll reduce it to five-hundred thousand," Cheatham said.

It seemed like he'd settled on the same amount the last time I'd appeared before him. I think Judge Cheatham might just be a half-million-dollar kind of guy.

"Are you ready to set a date for the preliminary?" he asked.

Biggs nodded. "Yes, your honor."

"Counselor?"

"As soon as possible."

"Well, then." He pulled over his calendar. "I've actually got Monday open. This won't take more than a day, will it?"

"It might," Biggs said.

Cheatham raised his eyebrows.

"There are some elements to this that make it more complicated than the run-of-the-mill case."

"I wondered why the district attorney himself was present at an arraignment."

I didn't know, but I was pretty sure it wasn't because he missed my pretty face.

"A day and a half?" Cheatham asked.

"Two days, I think. Depending of course on what kind of case the defense puts on."

When Cheatham looked at me, I smiled. "I'd hate to limit the defense's options at this point."

Cheatham rolled his eyes. "Okay. We could start Friday afternoon of next week, pick it up again the following Monday." He looked up from his calendar. "Unless you'd be ready to go Thursday of this week."

"The defense would be ready," I said.

Biggs nodded. "The prosecution would welcome an early date."

"Very well then. Thursday it is. We'll get started at nine a.m."

I said goodbye to Willow, and the deputy sheriff took her away. I turned toward the swinging gate in the bar and almost ran into Aubrey. He smirked up at me. "Counselor," he said.

"Mr. D.A. man."

"You are an arrogant thing, aren't you?"

I doubted he would have called a man an arrogant thing. "Just a pushy female who doesn't know her place," I said.

Cherchez la femme, Paul had said. Another good adage for detective work is *Follow the money*, though I think the phrase was originally used in connection with ferreting out corruption in politics. Since I had

Rodney Burns checking into Peyton Shilling, which was all I knew to do to cherchez la femme, I spent most of the day with Chris's financial records. They'd been occupying a bit of floor along the wall beside my desk. I'd kicked them nearly every time I'd gone around my desk, but had had no time to delve into them.

That afternoon I had a couple of folders open and papers spread over the desk when Carter Fox came in and sat uninvited in one of my client chairs. I opened a file folder on top of the exposed papers, which related to a limited partnership called South of Main. Carter nodded in the direction of the roses that I had moved to the credenza to give myself room to work. "I haven't seen much of you lately," he said. "You're still enjoying the roses, I trust?"

"Doesn't everybody enjoy roses?"

"Women do," he said. "That's what they say." His slick, black hair glinted in the overhead fluorescents.

"Do men not like flowers, you think, or are they just afraid of them? Too much of a threat to their masculinity?"

He licked his finger and drew a vertical line in the air, chalking one up for Robin Starling. "What did your boyfriend think of them?"

"Paul didn't seem to appreciate them all that much. Of course, he isn't female."

"I see he hasn't responded to the challenge with flowers of his own."

"I'm sure he will once he realizes what a turn-on they are."

Carter's eyes blinked, and the tip of his tongue appeared between his lips.

"I'm kidding, Carter. There's no magic button to push for sexual favors. The way it works is, you develop a relationship."

"Going to lunch, dropping by your office now and then for a few minutes of conversation? Sending flowers as a sign of one's esteem?"

"I do thank you for the flowers. They're very nice. And I appreciate your efforts at relationship-building, though right now I'm snowed."

"Representing that woman who killed her husband?"

"That woman falsely accused of killing her husband."

"You don't really think she's innocent."

"All my clients are innocent until proven otherwise. I think there was something about that in law school, but I'll have to check my notes."

Carter uncrossed his legs and stood up. "You're busy. I understand." He stopped in the doorway and looked back at me over his shoulder. "It's your fault, you know. You were sitting in here looking so cute behind your desk, I just had to drop in and say hello."

I gave him a nod. "Hello. And thanks again for the flowers."

When he was gone, Brooke came in, Carly right behind her, wide-eyed and curious. She glanced back toward the hall, then closed the door.

"He irritates the hell out of you, doesn't he?" Brooke said.

"He was just being friendly."

"Don't pretend. The man bought you flowers, probably set him back fifty or sixty bucks, and you were hardly civil to him. 'I think there was something about that in law school, but I'll have to check my notes.' "

I blew out a sigh. "You're right. He has the potential to turn into a problem, though."

Carly shuddered. "He's just so oily."

"He'll never get stuck in a drainpipe, that's for sure," I said.

Brooke and Carly only looked perplexed.

"He'd slide right out," I explained.

Their expressions cleared, though neither laughed or even cracked a smile. It seemed to me I used to be a lot funnier. "You can see Paul has nothing to worry about," I said. "You might mention that to him sometime, if it comes up in conversation."

"Oh, it comes up," Carly said.

"Hard for it not to, when he sees those roses every time he walks over," Brooke said.

Paul came over to my house for dinner that night. When we ate over at his place, he usually made a production of it, a white tablecloth on the table, a meal that took time and thought to prepare. When we ate at my house, we had salad with deli meat torn up on it, either turkey or chicken. We did have wine usually, or I did, while Paul had one of those dark beers that gave him what I'd come to think of as Paul-breath.

After dinner we took Deacon for his walk. It was dusk and hard to see. Soon it would be dark enough to make Deacon invisible. No neighbors had complained about him running loose, not yet, but I made an effort to stay aware of him—as aware as you can be of a dog who has disappeared into the gloom and is nowhere in sight.

R.E.M. began playing on my cell phone, and I slipped the phone out of my pocket. The screen showed a number I didn't recognize—hence the generic ringtone—but I answered anyway.

"Hello?"

There was a brief silence, then a child's voice. "Is dis Miss Wobin?"

"Caden? Yes, this is Robin."

"Is Dacon dare?" He pronounced Deacon's name so that it rhymed with *bacon,* but I got the idea.

"Yes, he's here. Would you like to speak to him?"

"Yes. I would wike to speak wif him."

"Let me call him for you." I put the cell down against my thigh. "Deeks!" I called. "Deeks, old buddy."

"I thought you were calling him Deacon now," Paul said.

"When I can remember. Deacon!"

Paul put his fingers to his mouth and gave a piercing whistle.

"He isn't trained to respond to a whistle," I said.

"I thought it might get his attention."

"Just a minute," I said into the phone. "Deacon's coming." And he was. It's difficult to say how I knew. It wasn't that I heard him pushing through brush or heard his toenails on the road. It was more like the charge in the air before a thunderstorm. Then I glimpsed movement on the other side of the road, and I held up my hand.

"Wait," I called, and Deacon halted in the dark grass just his side of the bar ditch. No cars were coming, but I didn't like him darting out into the road without giving me the chance to check it out. "Come," I said, and he jumped the ditch and crossed the road toward me. I squatted, and he gave my face a lick.

"Remember Caden?" I asked him. "The little boy who visited us?" Deacon looked like he was taking it all in, though I'm not so deluded as to think he understood any of it. "He wants to talk to you." Into the phone I said, "Caden? Are you still there? Here's Deacon. I'm holding the phone up to his ear." I did, leaning my head in to hear what Caden was saying.

"Hey, Dacon, it's me, Caden. Gammy and P-paw tooked me to da zoo taday. Dey was monkeys dare. Do you wike monkeys? I wike 'em—a wot! Dey so funny. Dey was a tigah dare, and he was big!" I expected Deacon to lose interest quickly, but he listened to a recounting of ewiphants and big bwack kitties and giwaffes and a hippapwatamus. Eventually, I heard a woman's voice in the background, then she came on.

"Robin? Are you there?"

"I'm here. I guess you took Caden to the zoo? He was telling Deacon and me all about it. If you want to put him back on, I'll see if I can get Deacon to say something."

"Here he is."

I turned the phone toward Deacon. "Speak," I said.

He looked at me.

"Speak!"

He gave a tentative woof.

"Good boy. Did you hear him? Deacon says hello."

"Dacon says hi to me," Caden said to someone. Deacon moved away from me a step, his eyes on my face.

157

I nodded. "Okay," I said.

He ran back across the street and disappeared behind the house. I know what you're thinking: There's no telling what he was getting into; dogs shouldn't be allowed to run loose. It isn't safe for them or for others, and it's no good saying how much he likes it. Believe me, I hear it all the time.

"We took him to the National Zoo. He's been before, but he didn't remember it at all," Gammy said.

"I can tell he had a good time."

"Yes. We all had a good time. How are things down there?"

"We had the arraignment today, but Willow's still in jail on bail of half-a-million dollars. The preliminary hearing starts Thursday."

"This Thursday?"

"Both the prosecution and I are trying to rush it."

"Why are you rushing it?"

"To find out what I can about the prosecution's case. I need something to work on."

The next morning I went by the Richmond City Jail to see Willow. In her orange jumpsuit her skin looked even paler than it usually did, and, in contrast to her jet black hair, that was pretty pale.

"So," she said in her throaty voice. "Preliminary hearing tomorrow."

"There's no jury," I said. "A district judge hears evidence and decides whether there's probable cause to hold you for trial in circuit court. It's not a high bar for the prosecution, but they will have to show most of their case."

"Will I be testifying?"

"No. The point is to take a look at the prosecution's case, not give them a look at ours."

"But at the main trial?"

"I don't know. You don't have any felonies or scandals in your past...at least not that I know of."

She shook her head.

"You might make a really good impression on the jury. I'll have to think about it."

"I just want to get home to Caden."

"I know. He is doing really well with his gammy and p-paw. He called me last night to tell me about it." I repeated what he'd said about his trip to the zoo.

"So why are you here?" she said finally. "Hold my hand a little, make me feel better?"

"How am I doing so far?"

She smiled, but sadly.

"Actually, I wanted to ask you about a limited partnership called South of Main. There was a slim folder devoted to it among your financial records."

She rolled her eyes. "Chris's folly."

"What do you mean?"

"I shouldn't complain. It might be what brought him back to me, but he did lose us a pile of money."

"Sixty thousand dollars, as near as I can tell," I said. Late last fall, twenty thousand dollars had been wired from their brokerage account into checking and another forty from Chris's retirement account. He'd written two checks to South of Main, LP, spaced about six weeks apart, in exchange for one-and-a-half shares of the limited partnership.

"Peyton Shilling got him into it," Willow said. "First, she and Chris bought a share of the partnership together, then he bought another one on his own."

"What does the partnership do?"

"Buys real estate between Main Street and Cary just south of the Fan District. Apartment buildings, rent houses, maybe a commercial property or two."

"Seems like a promising investment. What was wrong with it?"

"I don't know, but Chris seemed to feel like he'd been taken."

"Was he doing anything about it?"

She shrugged. "I went to community college for two semesters. It wasn't the kind of thing he bothered to explain to me."

"And you didn't ask."

"Things were difficult between us. I didn't press him," she said.

Peyton Shilling had gotten Chris to invest in South of Main, which suggested she was connected to it somehow. That was promising, I thought. Maybe I could cherchez la femme and follow the money at the same time. When I got back to my office, I went to the website of the State Corporation Commission and looked up South of Main. I learned three things: One, the limited partnership was inactive. Two, the address of its principal office was on South Davis Avenue, or had been. Three, the partnership's registered agent was Peyton Shilling. Cherchez la femme indeed.

The southern border of the Fan District was Main Street, a street which was itself largely commercial—a lot of bars and restaurants among the row houses. The block between Main and Cary Street was transitional. Though the Fan District itself had gone through gentrification way back in the 1970s, the area south of it had been transitioning for longer than I'd been in Richmond.

I leafed back through Chris Woodruff's file on South of Main and found the prospectus for it, along with a slick brochure featuring some of the properties it owned. I also gathered the paperwork relating to Chris's purchase of his shares, one share in his own name, the other in his and Peyton's. What I needed was anything that connected any of it to his murder. Chris felt like he'd been taken, which was a promising start…but only a start.

I put it all aside and pulled over a legal pad. "Motives for Murder" went at the top, underneath it, "1. Love gone bad." In that category I could put Peyton Shilling and Willow herself. Chris had a reputation as a womanizer, so there was also the possibility of a female as yet unknown. I wrote, "Peyton, Willow, Woman Unknown."

Next category: Jealous rage. Maybe Peyton had a boyfriend or even a husband who didn't take kindly to the fling that had been featured so prominently on social media. Or maybe the unknown woman had a husband or boyfriend, if there'd been one.

Third category: Money…And I didn't know where that one led me.

I got up and went into Rodney's office, where he sat slurping coffee and looking owlishly over the rim of the mug at his computer screen. "You're a noisy drinker," I observed. "I guess you've heard that before."

He shook his head. "Never. I guess I haven't had many women in my life."

It seemed like a slur upon my sex, but maybe I had brought it on us. "Did you ever find out whether Peyton Shilling is married or has been married?"

He nodded solemnly.

"She is, or she has been?" I asked.

"Neither."

That was disappointing. "Any past or current boyfriends?"

"Sure. The whole pattern of her romantic life is laid out for us on social media."

"Who's her current paramour?"

"A young man named Tanner. I can't remember his last name, but I think it starts with a B…" He shook his head. "I'll have to look it up for you."

"Could you make me a list of all her men, past and present?"

"Going back…"

"Say two years."

He nodded, and I left his office only to run immediately into Carter Fox, who seemed to be lurking in the common area of our little cul-de-sac.

"Go to lunch?" he said.

"I'm sorry. I've already made plans."

"The boyfriend who doesn't send flowers?"

"That would be the one."

"Tomorrow then."

"I'll be in trial Thursday and Friday. Preliminary hearing."

"Of course. Next week sometime."

He was a persistent bugger. "We'll see," I said.

"Fair enough." He looked at my legs, checked out my hips and my breasts on his way back up to my face. I gave him a sour look.

"Enjoy yourself?" I asked.

He smiled at me and cocked his head. "Any man would."

When he left, Brooke swung open her office door, which had been standing only half open. "What was that about?"

"Just Carter Fox mentally undressing me."

"That man gives me the creeps."

"Yes. Someday I'm going to have to beat the snot out of him. I can feel it coming on."

"Well, I want to be there when it happens."

"Want to go to lunch? I'm heading out to the 3 Monkeys. I've got to check out a business out that way."

"What about your plans with Paul?"

"Purely imaginary. They're having some kind of banquet at the Fed today, community outreach or something."

The 3 Monkeys is not a good lunch place for two women who want to keep their figures. Brooke had the chicken and waffles; I had the Monkey Burger, which is a bacon burger with blue cheese and avocado. To be fair, there were lighter items on the menu, but what's the point of going to a place like the 3 Monkeys if you're just going to have the garden salad?

"How do you eat like that?" Brooke asked me at one point when we both had our mouths full.

"I have a dog. Keeps me active."

"How do I eat like this?"

I swallowed. "An inefficient metabolism?" I suggested.

"Thank God for inefficiency."

After lunch we walked around the corner to South Davis. The address I had for South of Main was at the corner of South Davis and Cary Street. It was a row house with steps leading up to double doors inset with beveled glass. A metal plaque to one side of the doors said *South of Main, L.P.* but a black paper *For Lease* sign was taped to the inside of the glass. There was a phone number handwritten with a Marks-a-lot in the white rectangle, and I tapped the number into my phone as we walked back down to the sidewalk.

"Hello," I said to the woman who answered the phone. "My name is Robin Starling. I wanted to ask about the office space you have available on South Davis."

I turned as I spoke to look back at the house. Only the ground floor of the house appeared to be commercial, and I wondered who lived above it, if anyone. "I'm a little worried about the convenience of the location and the adequacy of parking and that sort of thing. It looks like the previous business didn't last long. Could you tell me how many businesses have been in the location in the last three to five years? Uh huh. The last one was called South of Main, some kind of limited partnership, I think. What kind of business were they in, do you know? Huh. Property management. No, I'm a lawyer. I assume the zoning would allow for a law office? How long was South of Main here? And its predecessor?"

By the time I was done, Brooke had settled herself on the low wall that held the small patch of rising lawn off the sidewalk. "Sorry," I said to her.

"It's okay, but I ate too much for lunch. I'm beginning to feel the need for either a nap or an afternoon cup of coffee."

"I'll get you back to the office, and we'll have coffee."

"So what did you find out?" she asked as we walked back down the street in the direction of my car.

"South of Main had a six-month lease, but moved out before the end of it."

"Any other useful information?"

"Not really. I mean, I learned a good bit about the property and it's suitability for a small law office—it would actually work pretty well, I think—but nothing that's going to help me at the preliminary hearing tomorrow."

"You're not thinking of moving your law office, are you?"

"No." I gave her a smile. "If I was, I'd be looking for space for you and Rodney Burns, too."

"Don't forget Carter Fox."

"Ah, yes," I said. "Who could forget him?"

When we got back to the Executive Suites, each of us got a mug of coffee, and we went to sit in Rodney's office across the desk from him.

He eyed us defensively, looking from one to the other of us. "Should I be worried?"

"I don't know," I said. "Have you got anything to hide?"

"Probably nothing you'd be interested in." He made a stab at a smile, but seemed too nervous to hold onto it.

"Try us," Brooke said. "Tell us about your love life. Where does a swinging single man of forty go to pick up women in this town?"

Rodney's eyes widened, and his gaze shifted, evidence of the fight-or-flight adrenalin being dumped into his bloodstream.

"Remember? He goes to Hooter's, chats up the waitresses," I said.

"That's right!" Brooke said. "I'd forgotten about that. Do you always sit at the same table? Is there a particular waitress you like?"

Rodney started rearranging the clutter on his desk, his breath coming faster.

"One thing I've always wondered," I said. "Do they have real names like Megan and Liz, or do they all use names like Honey or Brandy?"

"Or Candi with an *i*," Brooke said.

Rodney placed both palms flat on his desk in an apparent effort to hold them still. I thought he might make a break for it.

I held up a hand to forestall any escape attempt. "Really," I said. "We're just killing time while we drink our coffee. If I drew up a subpoena for you, do you think you could get it served this evening?"

His eyes shifted to meet mine. "Maybe," he said carefully.

"It's Peyton Shilling. You have her address. Actually, you're the one who gave me her address. You know, she's actually a very attractive female just a couple, three younger than us. She might be a possibility for you."

Brooke said, "Maybe you could get her to put on some short orange shorts and a cut-off T-shirt when you go over."

"I'll bet she has a pierced navel," I said.

Rodney's eyes had widened again, and again I held up a hand in a placating gesture. "I'm sorry. We can't seem to resist teasing you this afternoon. We'll go." I stood, and Brooke looked up at me.

"Do we have to? I'm having fun."

"Don't you have work to do?"

She looked at her watch. "Oh my gosh, I'm supposed to be on the Southside at three o'clock."

I smiled at Rodney. "I've got work to do, too. You're safe. I'll give you the subpoena before I leave this afternoon."

As I left, he cleared his throat, and I turned back to see his adam's apple bob in his thin neck. He didn't say anything.

As I crossed to my office, Brooke, purse in one hand and briefcase in the other, ducked back into his doorway to waggle her fingers at him. That was a bit much, I thought. It was in moments like this it occurred to me that maybe we weren't such nice people.

I spent some more time that afternoon on Chris's folder for South of Main. The glossy brochure showed three apartment buildings and a half-dozen row houses. I put it aside and picked up the prospectus that had been used to market shares in the company. The partnership's business plan was to buy houses and apartment buildings between Main and Cary and rent them out to create an income stream while the properties appreciated in value.

There were four property deeds in the folder. The deeds had legal descriptions rather than street addresses, so I got on the website for the city assessor's office and looked up the properties, writing the street addresses on sticky notes and pasting them to the deeds. Comparing the deeds to the properties featured in the glossy brochure, I saw that the deeds covered all three apartment buildings and one of the row houses.

I sat back and propped my feet on the edge of the desk. Sixty thousand dollars had gone into that limited partnership, money that Willow considered lost—and evidently Chris had, too. From the paperwork in his file, though, I didn't see the problem, certainly nothing that was going to help his widow in her murder trial. I reached for the folder again and dragged it over to take another look at the deeds. They all showed different grantors, which was not surprising. To put together a real estate portfolio, the limited partnership would have had to make purchases from a number of different owners. What was a more surprising was that the grantees were all different, too. There was no mention of South of Main on any of deeds. Were these copies of the deeds that South of Main had made in the process of making its purchases? How had the copies come to be in Chris's possession?

"Robin, I—"

I looked up. Rodney was in the doorway, his caterpillar mustache twitching as his mouth worked.

"Yes?"

His eyes cut down, and I realized I still had my feet on the edge of the desk and my chair tilted back. Given the length of my dress, my posture was possibly indecorous—possibly indecorous in the extreme. I took my feet of the desk and jolted forward.

"I'm sorry, Rodney, I was lost in thought. I didn't mean to be making a spectacle of myself."

He cleared his throat, his face reddening and his mustache continuing to twitch.

"Are you all right?"

"Yes. I, ah, I have some errands to run. I thought if you had that subpoena ready…"

"Oh, sorry. I got some blank ones from the clerk. Let me fill one in."

When he was gone, I took a big breath and exhaled it, still embarrassed about Rodney walking in on me. It could have been a lot worse, of course. It could have been Carter Fox who walked in on me.

Somehow, even that thought didn't make me feel better.

It was getting late in the day, late enough for me to begin to think about going home early, but the South of Main folder was bothering me. Instead of heading straight for my parking garage, I walked across downtown to the courthouse. One benefit of having on office a half-mile from the courthouse, I told myself as I trudged along in my sneakers, carrying my shoe bag as well as my briefcase, was that I did burn some calories from time to time.

The office of the circuit court clerk maintained the city's deed records in a vast library of low bookshelves with volume after volume of fat, oversized binders. All records beginning in 1993 were available online, just as you might expect, for anyone willing to pay the subscription fee of fifty dollars a month. For us more occasional users, there was the deed room.

I started with the grantee index and looked up South of Main, LP. There was one entry. I jotted down the recording information and walked through the shelves to the indicated volume. According to the deed, the South-of-Main property was on Allen Street. There was both a legal description and an address on this one. I got Chris's folder out of my briefcase. This wasn't one of the properties he had the deed to. The brochure did show a property on Allen Street, though, one side of a semi-attached house.

I went back to the grantee index and looked up South of Main again, but I hadn't missed anything. The only entry was for the one house on Allen Street. Where were the rest of the properties? For the sake of thoroughness, I tried "Main, South of," but there were no entries under that at all. I got out the four deeds that had been in Chris's folder and looked up the grantees in the grantor index: When and to whom they had conveyed the properties that had been conveyed to them?

Three of the grantees were there, having conveyed various properties in the City of Richmond at some point, but none of the conveyances covered the properties I had deeds to. From what the deed records showed, the grantees shown on the deeds still owned the properties featured in the brochure. None of them had conveyed any properties to South of Main. If South of Main had in fact acquired all the properties featured in its brochure, why hadn't it recorded the deeds?

At the very least, there'd been some sloppy management at South of Main. Possibly, there'd been something squirrelly going on—and that was encouraging. I could work with squirrelly.

When I came out of the courthouse, Detective Tom McClane was sitting on the low wall just this side of the sidewalk, an ankle crossed on his knee. He was leaning back on his arms in evident enjoyment of the balmy spring day.

"Ah, Starling," he said. "They said you were at the courthouse."

"Who said?"

He waved a hand. "Your friends at the Ironfronts, though everyone there seems very protective of you. They didn't want to tell me where you were. Why is that, Starling?"

"Did we have an appointment?" I asked him.

He laughed. "That's a good one. An appointment. No, no appointment. I was just dropping by to see you."

"And then you followed me to the courthouse."

"Well, sure. There was no point in walking around in there looking for you, though. I knew if you were in the courthouse, you'd be coming through that door eventually. I could just sit here and enjoy the sunshine until you did."

"So is this a friendly visit, or isn't it?"

"Oh it's a very friendly visit. I wanted to invite you along for a ride."

"You're going to take me for a ride? Where?"

"You can't guess?"

I threw open my hands in negation.

"Headquarters," he said. "I need someone to participate in a line-up, some woman who's tall and blonde, and I think you're just the woman who would do."

"Is what I'm wearing fine, or should I go home first to pick up a swim suit and an evening gown?"

His lip curled. Once again I had the impression that I wasn't as funny as I thought I was. "What you're wearing is fine," he said.

"My car's in a garage on Main Street."

"Oh, I'll give you a ride back to your car after the line-up—if you get to go back, that is."

I didn't like it. "I don't think so."

I started walking, but he was beside me before I reached the sidewalk. "I'm asking nice, but I can get a warrant," he said.

"You'll find me in my office."

"Have it your way." He stopped walking and I lengthened my stride as I headed toward Broad Street, internally debating the best course of action. I needed to be in court for the preliminary tomorrow, which might mean that I ought to make myself scarce until then. On the other hand, I'd received notice that the police were getting a warrant for my arrest, and I'd just committed to be in my office. Flight could be used as evidence of guilt...of what I didn't know, but McClane obviously thought I was guilty of something, and he thought he had the evidence to make it stick.

My pace slowed, and I looked back. He was still watching me. I turned around and went back. "Okay," I said. "Let's go to headquarters and get it over with."

Chapter 9

This was my second time to participate in a line up, which might mean I had the wrong sort of law practice. Certainly, I was the only lawyer I knew who had ever been put on display for potential witnesses. We took an elevator to the fourth floor and went around a corner, where McClane opened a door and ushered me inside. There was a female police officer present and four women seated along one wall. On the ride over, McClane had called ahead to say we were coming.

I took one of the two remaining chairs as he closed the door on us.

"Witness is on his way, or supposed to be," the police officer said to me. "But we may be a while."

"So the witness is a man?" I said.

"His or her way, I should have said."

I looked around at the other women, but the only one who made eye-contact immediately looked away. I didn't think any of them were as tall as I was, but they were probably all five-six or better, with blonde or strawberry blonde or light brown hair. One had twenty or thirty pounds on me, though the others were about my build. It might be as fair a line-up as the police could put together on short notice.

The door opened, and a woman I knew came in and sat beside me. "Hi, Robin."

"Laura." She was one of the administrative assistants in the homicide division. "We have to stop meeting like this."

She laughed. "It's quite an honor, really. You're the most famous lawyer in homicide."

It made me think of what Abraham Lincoln had said being tarred and feathered and carried out of town on a rail: If it weren't for the honor of it, I'd rather walk. "So do you do this often, or just when I'm in the line-up?" I asked.

"This is my third time—twice now with you, once with another freakishly tall female." She smiled. She could talk like that without giving offense because we were pretty much the same height.

"Well, I'm glad to see you. I don't guess you know what this is about."

She shook her head.

With a glance at the police officer, I said, "Or that you could tell me if you did."

She tilted her head, looking at me. "On another topic," she said.

"Yes?"

"I like your dress."

"I got it at Macy's, out at Regency Square Mall. Where'd you get your outfit?" Clothes shopping is a challenge for women our height. Laura looked like a fashion model. She was wearing gray slacks with knees that were actually at her knees instead of a couple of inches above them, I had noticed when she came in. Her turquoise blouse had sleeves that came past her wrists. She'd gotten both online, she said, from TTYA, an acronym that I recognized, fashion-challenged though I was: Taller Than Your Average.

We talked clothes, and time passed, and eventually a buzzer sounded. The police woman said, "Okay. They're ready for us."

"Do we get cards to read?" I asked.

"No cards this time. You sound like you've done this before."

"I think of it as my civic duty."

We walked into a room with a long mirror along one wall. We faced it, we turned left, we turned right, we walked out again. "You three can go," the police officer said, indicating Laura and two others.

"Till next time," Laura said to me.

"Let's hope for better circumstances."

It was another long wait. A female deputy sheriff came and went with the two other women who had been in the line-up, so both were evidently in custody. The police officer who remained with me looked as if she was getting as irritated as I was before McClane opened the door and came in.

"You can go," he told the police woman. "I'll take her."

"It's about time."

An assistant commonwealth attorney named David Miller was waiting for the elevator.

"Hi, David," I said. "What are you doing at police headquarters?" David was olive-skinned and had a full head of wavy black hair. Evidently I had chatted him up in a bar once, or vice versa, though I didn't remember it. I did remember opposing him in court.

"Working hard to stamp out crime," he said. "You've got a trial tomorrow I understand."

"A preliminary hearing. Are you handling it?"

"Nope. You drew the big guy again."

"Does he often handle prelims?"

"Never. He's doing it just for you."

"It's nice to be loved."

"They say love and hate are two sides of the same coin."

"I don't like that coin," I said. "I think I'd like to give it back."

David reached out his finger and swiped it down my nose. The elevator doors slid open, and the three of us got on, me, David Miller, and Tom McClane.

"What was that for?" I asked Miller. I swiped my finger along his nose, and he smiled.

"Keep it clean," he said.

McClane's car was in the parking garage. When we were in it and he had his arm hooked over the seat back to reverse out of his space, I said, "So don't keep me in suspense. Did your witness identify me or not?"

"I'm not arresting you, if that tells you anything. My instructions are to drop you back at your office or any place else you want to go."

I looked at my watch. It was 4:15. Images of home and Deacon beckoned me, but I had a trial tomorrow. "My office is fine."

We cut over to Cary Street and turned in the direction of downtown. I tried again. "It's not like you to be so reticent. Don't you want to gloat or anything?"

He glanced at me and stretched his mouth in something that was not quite a smile.

"Or maybe you're pissed off because I've somehow slipped through your fingers again."

He kept his eyes on the road and shook his head.

"Have it your way. Just remember that however it looks, I'm as pure as the driven snow. That thought will keep you on the path of righteousness."

He snorted, and I gave up.

The next morning events seemed to conspire against me. My mother called while I was running Deacon. Her ringtone is the theme music from the movie *Halloween*, which is uncharitable of me, I know. I must have been in a mood when I selected it, though I really don't remember. I dropped into a walk as I fished out my phone to talk to her. It's not that I don't like talking to my mother, but I was preoccupied with thoughts of trial. I forgot all about Deacon until I was nearly home.

"Deacon! Deacon, old buddy."

I listened but didn't hear anything. I retraced my steps for a block or so, looking out for him and calling, but with no result. I turned again and headed home. I didn't like it, but it wasn't the first time Deacon had gotten too interested in whatever he was doing to stay in voice range. When I went in to take my shower, I left the front door to the house standing open so Deacon could wander in when he got back, along with anyone else who might want to watch a woman shower.

I was out of the shower and picking out my underwear when he trotted in, tongue lolling, looking pleased with himself and sure of his welcome. I had an uneasy thought.

"It's time to get you fixed, isn't it?"

He looked up at me with a happy, trusting expression, and I rubbed the top of his head.

Anyway, by the time I'd dropped him off at Dr. McDermott's, I was running late, and I walked into the courtroom right at nine o'clock to see the gallery half-filled with spectators, Aubrey Biggs hunched at his table like a arthritic gnome, and Willow Woodruff alone at the defense table. The judge was not on the bench, but the court reporter disappeared through a door as I came in, and when he came back the judge was right behind him.

"Oyez, oyez, oyez..." Everyone stood as the bailiff called the court to order.

Judge Cheatham looked at me as he thumped his files on the bench. "Glad you could join us."

"Glad to be here, your honor."

He grimaced at my cheerful tone and sat. "We're here in case of Commonwealth vs. Willow Woodruff. The defendant is represented by Ms. Robin Starling; the Commonwealth is represented by Mr. Aubrey Biggs. Is the defense ready? Mr. Prosecutor?"

We were both ready.

"The charge is murder in the first degree. Will the defense waive the reading of the indictment?"

I waived it to make up for keeping the judge waiting.

"Mr. Biggs, do you have an opening statement?"

"No, your honor."

"Call your first witness."

I looked at my watch. It was 9:05, and we were already into it.

The prosecution's first witness was a police officer named Dub Ahern. He looked about thirty, his skin pale and freckled and his hair flaming red. He had been with the Richmond Police Department for five years.

"Have you ever seen the defendant Willow Woodruff before?" Biggs asked him.

"Yes, sir. I saw her on April 11."

"How did you come to meet her?"

"I went to her house as the result of a call from dispatch."

"What happened there?"

"She answered the door. She didn't say anything. She just opened the door for us and backed into the house, staring like, and she stopped by a doorway into a hall."

"When you say she opened the door for *us*..."

"My partner and me. Logan Fisher."

"And when she stopped by that doorway into the hall?"

"I said, 'In there?' or something like that, and she just kept staring."

"So what did you do?"

"Well, my partner Logan stayed with her, just kind of watching her, and I went into the hall. It was a short one with three doors opening off it. The one on the end to the left had the light on, so I went that way and found a man lying on the bed with blood all over the sheets and comforter. It looked like...well, I saw what I took to be a gunshot wound. There was an entrance wound on one side of his head and an exit wound on the other."

Willow's clenched right hand was just inside my field of vision, the knuckles whitening.

"Did you check to see if the man was alive, if he needed medical attention?"

Officer Ahern's mouth twisted. "No, sir. It was pretty obvious he was beyond help."

"Even to a nonprofessional like yourself?"

He swallowed, his adam's apple rising and falling. "There was all the blood, but more than that... the man's head had kind of lost its shape. It was distorted somehow."

I glanced at Willow, sitting rigidly with her fisted hands, holding on, but maybe not by much.

"What did you do?" Biggs asked Officer Ahern.

"I changed places with my partner, let him see what had happened while I called in the homicide. Then we all ended up in the living room while we waited for the M.E. and the detectives from homicide. Ms. Woodruff sat by herself on the sofa. She still hadn't said anything."

"Did she ever say anything?"

"Yes. She did say one thing." Ahern glanced at Willow, his tongue moistening his lower lip. "She said she had blood on her hands."

"Thank you, officer. Your witness."

I went to the podium. "Officer Ahern. Can you tell us whether Willow Woodruff did have blood on her hands?"

"You mean literally? You mean could I tell whether she'd killed her husband?"

"I do mean literally, but you're taking my question metaphorically."

"Ma'am?"

I had lived to be ma'amed by a cop. I held up my hand, the palm facing Officer Ahern. "Do you see my hand?"

"Yes, ma'am."

"Is there blood on it?"

"Not that I can see."

"So I don't have blood on my hand."

"No."

"Let me ask you again. When you saw Willow Woodruff in the early afternoon of April 11, did she have blood on one or both of her hands?"

"Oh, I see what you mean. Yes, I think she may have. And there was a streak of something that might have been blood on her cheekbone."

I asked a few more questions, but that was the big shining moment in my cross-examination of Officer Ahern. Aubrey Biggs might try to argue that Willow had made a confession, but I thought I had at least as strong an argument that, still dazed from finding her husband's body, she had simply noticed blood on her palm or on her fingers.

Biggs's next witness was a pathologist from the Office of Chief Medical Examiner, a man I hadn't encountered before, though he looked as though he'd been around since World War II. He took the witness stand in a rumpled lab coat with several strands of his dirty-gray comb-over hanging down past his left ear. He blinked at Aubrey Biggs through heavy-framed glasses.

"Dr. Murray. Could you tell us your full name please? And your occupation?"

He was Dr. Michael Murray, and he had been with the Office of Chief Medical Examiner for forty years.

Biggs walked him through the rest of his credentials, which included medical school at the University of Virginia and a pathology residency at Johns Hopkins. Dr. Murray didn't know how many autopsies he'd done—hundreds, maybe thousands.

"Did you have occasion to go to 4524 West Seminary Avenue on the afternoon of April 11?"

"Did I have occasion…yes. Yes, I did." His voice had a dusty, wheezy quality. "I was on-call that day."

"What did you find there?"

The doctor began to fumble with the papers in a folder. "I found," he began. "I found…ah, here we are. One Caucasian male, late twenties or early thirties, deceased. He was sprawled in a supine position on a full-size bed in one of the bedrooms."

"When you say sprawled…"

"He was sideways on the bed, legs hanging off, feet almost touching the floor."

"Did you make any preliminary determinations as to the cause of death?"

Dr. Murray blinked at him, his eyes magnified by thick lenses. "Gunshot wound," he said in his wheezy voice. "Gunshot wound to the head."

"Was it a contact wound?"

"No. Not a contact wound."

Biggs waited, but that seemed to be all of it.

"How do you know?" he said.

"The appearance of the wound."

Again Biggs waited. Finally, he said, "Could you possibly be more specific?"

The ghost of a smile touched Dr. Murray's mouth, almost as if he was messing with Aubrey Biggs and was enjoying it. "Yes, I could, possibly." But he made us wait while he cleared his throat and worked his mouth to moisten it. "There wasn't any of the tearing and peeling of the skin that you find when a gun is fired at a range closer than about twelve inches. There wasn't the muzzle print or the star pattern you'd expect from a contact wound."

"So what was the distance of the shot?"

"Between twelve and thirty-six inches, probably toward the upper end of that range. There was a little tattooing from the particles of burning gunpowder, but not much."

Biggs nodded, swallowed, took a breath. "What do you estimate was the time of death?"

"Time of death. Let's see." Dr. Murray flipped through a couple of pages, then flipped back to what may have been the same place he started. "I saw the body at 2:22. The decedent had been dead at that point..." He flipped back a page. "...between six and eight hours.

"So the time of death was between 6:22 and 8:22," Biggs said.

The doctor blinked, once, twice. "Approximately."

"On what do you base this determination?"

Dr. Murray closed his folder and sat back with it resting on his crossed legs. "Oh, a number of things." He looked around the courtroom, then seemed to realize we were waiting for him to elaborate. "Body temperature, rigor mortis, contents of the stomach," he said. "You know."

Biggs's smile looked pained. "Whatever we know or don't know, we have to get it in the record."

"Oh, quite right."

"The body was transported to the Office of Chief Medical Examiner, and you performed the autopsy, is that right?"

"Yes, my autopsy began…" He uncrossed his legs and reopened his folder. We watched him flip pages. "At 4:44."

"Did you recover a bullet from the decedent's body?"

"No, I didn't. There was an exit wound, quite a large one really. The bullet would have remained at the scene."

"And there was just the one gunshot wound?"

"Yes, just the one."

"Did the police subsequently give you a bullet for analysis?"

They did. Biggs presented it to him. The doctor identified it. Biggs got it marked for identification.

"What kind of analysis did you perform on the bullet?" he asked.

"We compared the DNA profile of blood traces found on the bullet with blood samples from the body of the decedent Christopher Woodruff. They were a match."

Biggs rolled his head in my direction and gave me a look that suggested now it was my turn to suffer. "Your witness," he said.

I stood. "Dr. Murray, I see you've been using some papers to refresh your memory. Are these notes you made at the time you made the observations recorded in those notes?'

He nodded. "It is contemporaneous documentation."

"May I see the notes?"

The doctor looked at Judge Cheatham, then looked at me. "I suppose so," he said.

The judge motioned in my direction with his head, and his clerk got up, retrieved the folder, and brought it to me at the podium.

I glanced through the notes. Though Dr. Murray had written all his numerals clearly, the rest of his handwriting was a messy scrawl. I'd gotten the actual autopsy report at the arraignment. If there was anything new here, I couldn't make it out. I closed the folder and held it up. "I'm done with it."

The judge jerked his head at me, and I took it back to Dr. Murray.

"When you say the DNA was a match, what do you mean?" I asked.

"I mean that the VNTR loci were the same."

"Do tell."

Dr. Murray chuckled, but it turned into a cough that sounded richly productive. He pulled out a wadded handkerchief and held it to his mouth.

"What does VNTR stand for?" I asked when he had recovered himself.

"Variable number tandem repeats."

It just got better and better. "Tell me about variable number tandem repeats," I said.

"They are highly variable DNA sequences that are unlikely to be the same between unrelated persons."

"So if Chris Woodruff had a brother, they might be the same?"

"They might be very similar. If he had a monozygotic twin, they would be the same."

"Monozygotic. Would that be an identical twin?"

"It would."

I'd been into the weeds on DNA profiling before. Though I didn't think it would get me anywhere, I spent the next forty-five minutes or so going into them again, and I was right. It didn't get me anywhere. With RLFP analysis—don't ask—the theoretical chance of a coincidental match was perhaps as little as one in 100 billion.

"But," I said. "You said that twins would have matching DNA profiles, and identical twins make up roughly point-two percent of the population."

The doctor nodded benevolently.

"Isn't that right, doctor?"

He cleared his throat. "That is correct."

We talked a bit about the number of available markers and eventually got the probability of a coincidental match up to one in a thousand, which was still not high enough to do me any good, even before a jury. "Are you familiar with a literature survey by William Thompson published in the Journal of Forensic Medicine?" I asked.

"I can't say that I am."

"So you're not aware that proficiency tests conducted by various forensic laboratories have found the occurrence of false positives to be as high as one in a hundred, or even two in one hundred?" A false positive was the finding of a match when in fact the samples came from two different people.

He shook his head. "I wouldn't put too much weight on those proficiency tests."

"So it doesn't matter to you that, in addition to coincidental matches that may occur one time in a thousand, laboratories mishandle samples and misinterpret results?"

"Objection, your honor," Biggs said. "That's an entirely improper question."

"It goes to bias, your honor."

"Ms. Starling," Judge Cheatham said.

He seemed to be waiting for a response. "Yes, your honor?"

"Do you really think there is any possibility that the bullet found on the scene was not the fatal bullet?"

I shrugged. "I have no way of knowing. We have an expert witness on the stand, and I'm using him to explore the evidence."

"Well, let's not spend any more time on it here. This is a preliminary hearing. I don't know what your theory of the case is, but even if you get the chance of a false positive up to one in fifty, I'm going to bind the defendant over for trial. You may have greater success with this line of argument in front of a jury."

I took a breath and blew it out through puffed cheeks. "Very well, your honor." I flipped back through my yellow pad of notes, then looked up at Dr. Murray.

"The amount of tattooing caused by a discharging firearm depends a great deal on the weapon, doesn't it?" I asked. "The length of the barrel, the condition of the weapon—that sort of thing?"

"Yes," he said, nodding. "It depends a great deal on both factors."

"How does it depend?"

He cleared his throat. "In general, the longer the barrel, the greater the distance at which tattooing will occur."

"So to tattoo the skin, a pistol would have to be closer than a rifle."

"Yes, it would."

"The prosecution hasn't introduced its murder weapon yet, but did the police ever give you a handgun to test tattooing patterns at different ranges?"

"No. That's not the sort of testing I do."

"Who does do that sort of testing?"

"I think some ballistics experts at various police departments might do it. I've never heard of anyone at the Richmond Police Department doing it."

"Doesn't the condition of the weapon have something to do with the range at which tattooing would occur?"

"The effect of the weapon's condition would be more variable."

"But could still be significant?"

"Of course."

I waited, then finally said, "So, given these factors, and in the absence of any testing of the murder weapon itself, the best you can give us is a firing range of one to three feet."

His eyes cut to his folder. He looked up. "That's why I gave it to you." He showed us a mouthful of mottled, yellow teeth.

I took a breath. As far as I knew, none of this mattered at all to Willow's case either. I'd pushed for an early preliminary to try to get a picture of what had happened, though, and of how tight the prosecution's evidence was. I was trying to make the most of my opportunity.

"You say Chris Woodruff had been dead between six and eight hours," I said. "In other words, he died at 7:22, give or take an hour."

Dr. Murray opened his folder to fumble with his notes again. "Yes," he said finally. "7:22 is about right."

"Give or take an hour."

"Always give or take."

"You mentioned the contents of the stomach as a determinant of the time of death. What were the contents of the stomach?"

"There weren't any."

"Telling you Mr. Woodruff had not yet eaten that morning?"

"He had not eaten for at least twelve hours. There was no food in his stomach and no food in his small intestine."

"That doesn't narrow the time of death much, does it? He could have been a late sleeper, or he could have gotten up early. He could have had an early supper or a late supper the night before, at least as far as you know of your own knowledge." I glanced at Biggs, wondering if he had a witness to testify as to the time of Woodruff's last meal.

"Certainly."

"All you can tell us is that he hadn't eaten that morning."

He blinked his deep set eyes. "I believe that's exactly what I said."

"How about his bladder? Was it full?"

"It was not."

"Had the bedding, was it…" I was conscious of Willow listening to this, but deliberately avoided glancing in her direction.

"It had not been soiled, no."

"So he did get out of bed that morning, at least to use the bathroom."

"It seems probable that he had used the bathroom."

"And he'd gone back to bed."

"Well." He glanced in Biggs's direction.

"Well? Had he gone back to bed or not?"

"He wasn't in the bed. He was just on it."

"What does that mean?"

"Well, he was sideways on the bed and on top of the rumpled sheets and the comforter. He was wearing only the boxers and T-shirt he might have slept in."

The scenario that was shaping up wasn't quite as I had pictured it. "Doctor…is it possible that Chris Woodruff was not lying in bed when he was shot, but that he was standing and fell back onto his bed?"

"I would say it's likely."

"On what do you base that opinion?"

"The pattern of blood spatter."

Blood spatter. "Where exactly was the entrance wound?" I asked. "What part of the head?"

"The left temple. The bullet punched through the sphenoid bone and exited behind the right ear, shattering parts of the parietal and occipital bones."

The names of the bones didn't mean much to me, but I got the idea. "What was the trajectory of the bullet? Upward, downward…"

"Slightly upward."

"If he was shot by someone the same height as he was, the gun might have been held at shoulder height?"

"Might have been. Of course, we don't know the angle of the decedent's head. It could have been back or bent forward."

"How tall was the decedent?"

"Five-ten."

"You mentioned several factors relevant to the time of death: Rigor mortis, livor mortis, and—"

"Algor mortis. The three mortises."

I heard a sound from the prosecutor's table, as if Biggs had dropped something or thrown something down, but Dr. Murray was smiling, showing his yellow teeth again, and his eyes had taken on a far-away look. "I wrote a poem about them once, back in med school." In his dusty voice he recited, "'Rigor mortis tells the time of death. Livor, if the body has been moved. Algor gives the time of death improved.'" His gaze focused. "I won't bore you with the rest of it. Frankly, in this case I relied mostly on that last one."

I glanced at Aubrey Biggs, who was sitting with his ankles crossed and his eyes on the ceiling. "You relied mostly on algor mortis to estimate the time of death in this case," I said.

"Oh, absolutely."

I felt like I was chasing down a rabbit hole, but I said, "Algor mortis is…"

"The cooling of the body after death."

"How fast does a body cool?"

"It depends."

"Can we start with an average?"

"One-point-five degrees per hour."

"Until?"

"Until it matches the ambient temperature."

"The temperature of the surroundings."

"Yes."

"Doesn't that depend in part on what the temperature of the surroundings is?"

"Yes, yes it does. Of course it does."

"And the temperature of the surroundings in this case was…"

"Seventy-four degrees."

"At 2:22 on the afternoon of April 11."

"That's right. The temperature at that time matched the setting of the thermostat, so I assumed that the ambient temperature was constant over the relevant time period."

"The rate of cooling depends on other factors, too, doesn't it? Clothing, baseline temperature, hydration, percentage of body fat…"

"Oh, yes. It's not precise. That's why I gave you a two-hour range for time of death rather than try to pinpoint it exactly."

"Because you can't pinpoint it exactly."

"No, I can't."

"Can you even get it within two hours? There's a temperature plateau, isn't there? The body doesn't begin to cool immediately."

"That's right. The body continues to produce heat for a short time after death."

"And that plateau can last anywhere from two to six hours."

"Yes."

"What was the temperature of the body at 2:22?"

For that he took another look at his notes. "Eighty-nine degrees."

"This was a core temperature?"

"Yes. I made a small incision in the decedent's abdomen and inserted the thermometer into his liver to take the reading."

"And you assumed that his baseline temperature was what?"

"Ninety-eight point six."

"That's a guess, isn't it? Doesn't the temperature of healthy people vary by a degree or more? Mr. Woodruff's normal temperature might have been as low as 97.6 and as high as 99.6."

"Yes, that's possible."

"You've suggested that the rate of cooling is linear, but it isn't, is it? There's the temperature plateau, then the body begins to cool rapidly, then the rate of cooling slows down."

He blinked at me. "You've been reading," he said.

"It keeps me out of bars."

There was a light titter from somewhere in the gallery, but the judge didn't react to it.

"Well, you're right of course," Dr. Murray said. "The linear formulation is an approximation."

I continued asking about the reliability of body temperature in determining the time of death and thought I'd gone a long way to challenging the last line of his little ditty, that 'Algor gives the time of death improved.' After I'd finished with algor mortis, I questioned the doctor about rigor mortis and postmortem lividity. Neither did much to narrow the likely range for time of death.

"I don't think you've managed to establish a two-hour window for the time of death," I said finally. "From what you've told us, it sounds like all we can say with any certainty is that Christopher Woodruff had been dead between three and twelve hours."

He shrugged. "What I've given you is my opinion."

I nodded abstractedly. Broadening the window didn't help me anyway, at least not that I could see. If I could *shift* the window, if I could show that Chris Woodruff had died after Willow left for work, that would be nice. Of course, world peace would be nice, too.

"Those are all my questions," I said, and I left the podium.

The prosecution's next witness was Detective Tom McClane. He came forward wearing a white shirt, black pants and a black tie, his badge clipped to his belt. After being sworn in, he stepped into the witness box, adjusted the crease in his slacks, and sat forward on his chair.

Biggs ran him through the preliminaries, his name and rank, educational background, years on the police force, number of homicide investigations, and so forth. "Did you have occasion to go to the residence at 4524 West Seminary Avenue on the afternoon of April 11?"

He did have such an occasion. After being notified of a possible homicide by the dispatcher, he and his partner Matt Tarrant had gone to that address and had arrived shortly before two o'clock.

"What did you find there?"

Officer Dub Ahern had opened the door for them, and McClane had seen the defendant Willow Woodruff seated in the living room with Ahern's partner Logan Fisher. When he'd gone back into the bedroom, he found the same thing Officer Dub Ahern and Dr. Murray had, a dead man sprawled on a full-sized bed.

"Had Dr. Murray arrived from the Office of Chief Medical Examiner when you got there?"

"No. He was fifteen or twenty minutes behind us."

"What did you do?"

"I called for a forensics team to examine the crime scene."

"Do you know of your own knowledge whether the forensics team recovered a bullet?"

"Yes. There was a 95-grain bullet imbedded in the wall about six-and-a-half feet above the floor."

"Just the one bullet?"

"Just the one. It had traces of blood on it. We sealed it in an envelope, and a couple of us wrote our names across the seal. Later I turned it over to the Office of the Chief Medical Examiner for DNA analysis."

"What caliber gun would have fired such a bullet?"

"It was a .380."

"Was there such a gun at the scene?"

"There was not."

"Did you subsequently recover such a gun?"

"I did. We retrieved a .380 Smith and Wesson Bodyguard from a trashcan at a Valero gas station out on Parham Road."

"Tell us about that gun."

"It was registered to the defendant, Willow Woodruff, and ballistics tests showed it to have fired the bullet I've just been talking about."

"The bullet that was recovered at the scene of the murder?"

"That's right."

"Was this gun—we'll call it the Willow gun—the first gun you tested as a possible murder weapon?"

"No, it was the second. The first was a handgun given to me by Robin Starling, the defendant's attorney."

Biggs turned his head to look at me, pursing his lips and looking thoughtful. He said to McClane, "Tell us about that gun."

"It was another Smith and Wesson Bodyguard that was identical to the murder weapon in every respect."

"Who was that gun registered to?"

"The decedent in the case, Christopher Woodruff. Evidently, the two guns had been purchased at the same time about two years ago."

McClane produced the registration papers. Biggs got them admitted into evidence, then asked, "Did the defendant's attorney make any statement about how this second gun, the Christopher gun, had come into her possession?"

"She said it came in the mail."

"It came in the mail," Biggs repeated.

"Then when we went to pick it up, it had disappeared."

"Disappeared?"

"Later it reappeared in her bedroom. At least, that's what she told us when she finally turned it over to us."

"Reappeared in her bedroom." Again Biggs turned his head to look at me. Judge Cheatham was looking at me, too, with apparent interest, which I took to be a bad sign. "Did she say how it came to disappear in the first place?" Biggs asked.

"No. She opened an empty drawer in her office and said it was gone. She didn't give any explanation."

"Did you ask her for one?"

"I did."

"And then she said the gun had reappeared, and she gave you the Christopher gun, the one that was not involved in the murder."

"That's right."

"When did you arrest the defendant in this case?"

"When we found the Willow gun in the trashcan. We discovered that it had fired the fatal bullet and was registered to the defendant."

"Were there any restraints on the defendant's movements during the time the gun was unaccounted for?"

"No."

"Were you keeping her under surveillance?"

"No."

"And certainly you weren't keeping the defendant's attorney under surveillance."

"Of course not."

"So during that time, based on the facts as you know them, it would have been possible for the defendant and her attorney to be passing the murder weapon back and forth between themselves before one or the other of them tried to dispose of the gun by throwing it into the trashcan at that Valero station."

I stood. "Objection. Leading and calls for speculation."

"It calls for a conclusion," Biggs said, contradicting me. "We have qualified the witness as an expert."

"In interpreting crime scenes maybe," I said. "He hasn't been qualified as an expert in all the things Willow Woodruff and I might have done in our spare time over the last couple of weeks. Ask the witness if it would have been possible for us to have been picking up men in bars or playing on the train tracks or composing a symphony. He'd have to give exactly the same answer to any of those questions."

Judge Cheatham rolled his eyes toward Biggs. "She has a point," he said.

"Your honor, the facts speak for themselves."

"Then we'll let them speak, why don't we, and not ask the witness to speak for them."

"Very well." Biggs closed the folder and opened another one on top of it. After flipping through some pages, he glanced at the clock. "Your honor, it's nearly twelve. I think I'm going to be some time with this witness."

The judge looked at the clock, hesitated a moment, then nodded. "All right. We'll recess until two o'clock."

I said a few words to Willow, and the deputy sheriff took her by the arm and led her out. A couple of attorneys who'd been waiting in the gallery came forward with a motion they wanted to put before the judge. Peyton Shilling pushed through the bar and approached Biggs, who was still organizing his papers and filing them in his briefcase.

I remained seated at my table, watching.

Peyton handed a document to Biggs that looked like the subpoena I'd prepared and given to Rodney to serve on her. Probably more trouble was brewing, but there didn't seem to be much I could do about it. I got up to push out through the bar, wondering if I'd made a mistake in forcing her to appear. She was a potential suspect. On the other hand, her affair with Willow's husband gave Willow a textbook motive for murder.

I'd have liked to talk it over with someone, and usually when I'm in trial I have friends around me. Paul or Brooke, even Mike McMillan, come to watch the trial, and we confer during breaks and go to lunch together. Today though, Paul was tied up at the bank, and Brooke had gone to Fredericksburg to look over a potential client's computer systems. I didn't know where Mike was. I was on my own—or so I thought until I got to the railing that separated the gallery, and

Carter Fox stood, smiling, and moved toward the aisle.

Chapter 10

I wasn't up for dealing with Carter Fox. I held up a finger, smiling, and turned back, letting the gate swing shut behind me. There were two other exits to the courtroom: one, a side exit through which the deputy sheriff had taken Willow; and two, the door behind the bench that the judge used, though others used it, too—the court reporters and judges' clerks for example. I went that way, overtaking the court reporter in the doorway. He was a gaunt man in his twenties with thinning, pale brown hair and almost colorless eyes.

"May I help you?" he said. The judge was still on the bench, conferring with the two lawyers and paying no attention to us.

"Yes, I hope so. Could we?" With a motion of my head, I indicated the hall beyond the door.

"Sure." We moved through the doorway into a short hall with more doors opening off it into offices—judges' chambers—and at one end an open door to a larger space that was the office of the district clerk. Though I'd visited judges in their chambers before, I did always have the feeling of having forgotten my hall pass.

"Actually, there's a man out there I'm hoping to avoid. Is there a back way out? I'm Robin Starling, by the way."

"Peter Davidson," he said, taking my offered hand. His own had a skeletal feel to it. "I think I can help you. If you go this way, you'll wind your way through the clerk's office and end up in the lobby right in front of the main door to the courtroom. On the other hand, that door at the other end opens into a hallway that leads to a back staircase."

"That would be perfect. Thanks."

There are easier things than going down a flight of stairs in heels, so I sat on the top step to switch out my pumps with the sneakers in my shoe bag. On the ground floor, I still had to go out through the main lobby to the front doors, but Carter Fox was nowhere in evidence. I felt a pang of guilt at the thought of him waiting in the courtroom for a lunch date that would never materialize—though maybe I was flattering myself, maybe he just wanted to pass on a few words of encouragement—but I squelched the guilty feeling and pushed out through the revolving doors.

The question was what to do next. I wasn't really hungry for anything, and my usual haunts were across downtown. I needed fuel, though, so I walked over to the convention center and got a salad with grilled chicken. Having a salad for lunch would allow for a bigger supper in the event that a day in trial put me in need of comfort food, which for me was on the order of a burger and a milkshake.

Though I didn't think the prosecution's case was particularly strong so far, it was hard to say the preliminary hearing was going well for Willow and me. Chris had been killed with Willow's gun in their home in his boxers. There was no evidence of anyone else having been in the house or even having access to the house. I'd left Peyton Shilling hobnobbing with Aubrey Biggs, probably telling him all about her affair with Chris, assuming he hadn't known already.

I ate my salad, chewing methodically, sipping from my cup of water, idling watching the conventioneers around me with their lanyards and badges. Eventually, I had an idea and dug out my phone.

I punched Rodney's name on my favorites list.

"Rodney Burns," he said.

"Hello, Rodney Burns. What are you doing right now?"

"Robin? Have you been drinking?"

I laughed, feeling suddenly better. "No, just thinking. I'm in court for Willow Woodruff's preliminary hearing. Well, right now I'm at lunch, but…"

"How's it going?"

"So so. Have you ever heard of the South of Main limited partnership?"

"No, I can't say that I have."

"It's the only loose end I can think of to tug on. I've been on the web, looked around at their properties…It bothers me that I haven't been able to find any of them in the deed records. Actually, I did find one property, but that just confirms I know to use the record books in the deed room. Anyway, Chris Woodruff was one of the limited partners in South of Main. The general partner is a corporation of some kind, though I can't remember its name." I paused for breath.

"Uh huh," Rodney said.

"Do you have some time this afternoon to go to the Corporation Commission, get copies of whatever documents there are about the limited partnership? Documents about the general partner, too, and anything else that seems of interest."

"Sure."

"The odds are pretty good of our getting paid, I think."

"Oh, well then. Definitely."

I ignored the sarcasm. "Good. See what you can find. If you leave for the day before I get back, get Carly to let you in my office and leave the papers on my desk."

"Roger Wilco."

I punched off, smiling. I liked Rodney.

At two o'clock, Tom McClane returned to the witness stand. "Officer McClane," Biggs said. "Tell us how you came to be digging in a trashcan at the Valero gas station out on Parham Road."

"We got a tip, an anonymous phone call to police headquarters."

"Did you manage to trace the call?"

McClane smiled. "We checked our phone records. The call came from the pay phone just off the food court at Regency Square Mall."

"Was it made by a man or a woman?"

"Man. At least, that was the notation made by the officer who took the call."

I half-stood. "Objection. Hearsay."

Biggs smiled. "The answer may be stricken. I'll even withdraw the question. Officer McClane, a call came in, and as a result of that call, you went out to a gas station on Parham Road. You personally?"

"Yes. Matt Tarrant, my partner, and I went. We found the gun in the second trashcan we checked."

"Where was this trashcan?"

"At the pump island with pumps five through eight."

"What day was this?"

"April the 18th, right at twelve noon."

"What did you do after you found the gun?"

"We bagged it, then went into the store to talk to the clerk."

"What did you learn from the clerk?"

I stood. "The question seems to call for hearsay."

Biggs said to McClane, "Did you ask whether he had observed a woman matching the description either of the defendant or her attorney at any of the pump islands that morning?"

"Objection. Leading." Lawyers weren't supposed to ask their own witnesses questions in a way that suggested the answer.

"Sustained."

Biggs took a breath. "Officer McClane, did the clerk give you a description of anyone he had been seen at any of the pump islands that morning?"

"He did not. The clerk couldn't even describe anyone who had been in the store that morning."

"So what did you do next?"

"We asked to see the records of that morning's credit transactions. It took a bit of doing. The clerk had to bring in the store manager, and the store manager had to bring in the district manager, but eventually we got them."

"And then?"

"We contacted some of the people on the list."

"Not all of them."

"No. We struck pay dirt on our second call."

"To whom was that call made?"

"Colton Jeffries."

"He had purchased gas that morning?"

"Yes, he had. At pump number eight."

"Did you subsequently conduct a lineup of people for Mr. Jeffries to identify?

"I did."

"Who was in the line up?"

McClane looked at his notes. "Six women under the age of forty ranging in height from five-six to five-eleven."

"Did Mr. Jeffries identify any of these women as a person he had seen at the Valero station?"

"He did."

"Thank you, Officer McClane. Those are all my questions at this time."

Biggs had fashioned a big ol' mud ball and was about to fling it my way, but for the moment I ignored it. I had a lot of ground to cover. I started with the crime scene—the body, the blood evidence, the 95-grain bullet embedded in the wall. I followed the chain of custody for the blood and the bullet. I walked him through the ballistics tests that had been done on the fatal bullet and the test bullets that had been fired both from the gun I had given him and the gun recovered at the Valero station. He presented photographs made with a comparison microscope, and I took some time to look at them.

"How about fingerprint evidence?" I asked him. "Did you check for fingerprints at the Woodruff home?"

"Of course."

"Did you find any that didn't belong to one of the Woodruffs?"

"We did not."

"Did you check for fingerprints on the two semiautomatic pistols you've been talking about?"

"We did. There weren't any. Both guns seemed to have been wiped clean after they were last handled."

"You didn't find my fingerprints, did you?"

"No."

"Not even on the pistol I gave you, the one you've been calling the Christopher gun?"

"You presented it to us in a plastic bag. Either you'd been careful about handling it, or you had wiped it clean."

"You didn't find Willow's fingerprints on either gun? Not even on her own gun?"

He hadn't.

"Did you check for gunshot residue on her hands and forearms?" When a gun is fired, gunshot residue particles are emitted from the back of the weapon as well as from the muzzle. It sticks to the skin and is almost impossible to wash off.

He shifted in his chair. "She was checked."

"But you didn't do the testing?" I said.

"I did not."

"Do you know the results?"

Biggs said, "Objection. Calls for hearsay."

I nodded, frowning at McClane. "Had you yourself discharged a firearm in the previous twenty-four hours?"

"I had qualified with my firearm during my prior shift." So there was the possibility of contamination, I thought.

"Where was the defendant tested? At the scene?"

"She was."

"Gunshot residue would have been present on the victim's body, wouldn't it, given the range from which the shot was fired?"

He nodded. "I imagine."

"The body wasn't tested for residue?"

"I didn't test it."

"Officer Ahern testified about blood on the defendant's hands. That would mean she had been in contact with the body, wouldn't it?"

"I don't know."

I had some work to do here before trial. I needed to get particle counts, a breakdown of the residue on Willow's arms and hands, maybe information about the composition of the residue that would be produced by the particular ammunition found in the pistol.

"When you found the handgun in the trashcan, was it loaded?"

"There were five rounds still in the clip."

"How many would it hold if it were fully loaded?"

"Six, plus one in the chamber."

"Had the weapon been fired recently?"

"It had been fired since it was last cleaned."

"Can you tell us how long it had been in the trashcan?"

"The clerk told us…" Biggs stood, and McClane stopped. "No," he said. "I can't."

"Did you ask the clerk when the trashcan had last been emptied?" I asked.

"Yes. I did."

I was thinking it would have been early that morning, but for confirmation and an approximate time I was going to have to talk to the clerk. Not that it mattered. I knew how long the gun had been there.

"What was the name of this clerk?"

McClane gave it to me, and I wrote it down.

"How full was this trash barrel where you found the gun?"

"Halfway. Two-thirds."

"What was in it other than the pistol?"

McClane shrugged. "Trash."

Someone in the gallery thought that was funny, judging by the sudden bray of laughter.

I suggested, "Cups, fast food sacks…"

"There was a bag from McDonalds. Some grocery bags full of trash and some drink cups. A lot of little stuff.

"Was the handgun resting right on top of all this?"

"No. It had worked its way to the bottom."

"Or perhaps it was thrown in first," I suggested. "Right after the trash was last emptied. Isn't that a possibility?"

"No. Based on what our witnesses told us…"

"As far as the physical evidence of the trashcan goes, the gun could have been thrown in first," I said.

McClane shrugged again. "I suppose it could have."

"Let's talk a little about this lineup you did. I take it that you yourself conducted it?"

"I did."

"You had a suspect, didn't you? Someone you suspected of disposing of the gun at the Valero station."

"Naturally."

"Are you aware that Department of Justice guidelines call for lineups to be conducted by someone who does not know the suspect?" Since appearing in McClane's lineup as the suspect du jour, I'd done a little reading up on the subject.

McClane glanced away from me, then back. "I am aware that there are conflicting opinions on how to conduct a lineup."

"Was this a sequential lineup or a simultaneous lineup?"

"Simultaneous."

"Are you aware that some studies find that the simultaneous lineup leads to more false positives than sequential lineups where the witness is presented with potential suspects one at a time?"

"Yes, and I'm aware that other studies show that simultaneous lineups are more accurate."

"Was the attorney for the defense present with you and the witness during the lineup?"

His lip curled. "She was not. Under the circumstances—"

I stopped him with a raised hand. "After the witness made his identification, did you ask him his degree of confidence?"

"I did."

"And?"

"He said he was pretty sure."

"Pretty sure? Did he subsequently become more confident in his identification?"

"You'll have to ask him. I think he did."

"After you encouraged him in his identification, or possibly even confirmed it?"

"I don't think so. Again, you'll have to ask him."

"He's the only one to ask, isn't he, since no one else was present as a witness to how the lineup was conducted."

"There was a uniformed officer present, an Officer Hill."

"What is Officer Hill's first name?"

"John."

I made a note of it. "Did you warn the witness that the person he'd seen at the Valero station might not be in the lineup?"

"I don't remember. I think I probably did."

At some point, I'd be arguing that the lineup was tainted, and McClane had given me at least some ammunition. "Thank you, detective. That will be all."

Biggs next witness was Colton Jeffries, a big, rangy guy with short brown hair who came to the stand wearing Wranglers and a striped shirt with the cuffs turned up. Biggs got his name and address along with his age, education, and occupation. He was twenty-six, had a B.B.A. in information systems, and worked as a process-controls engineer at Phillip Morris.

"Do you remember buying gas at the Valero station on Parham Road on the day of Friday, April 18?" Biggs asked him.

"Sure."

"When was that? What time of day?"

"Sometime in the morning. I'd been out at corporate headquarters and was headed back to the manufacturing plant."

"Would this have been around 10:16?"

The corner of his mouth turned up. "I understand that was the time stamp on my receipt, so I guess it must have been."

"You kept a copy of this receipt?"

"Yeah, I found it in my truck." He produced it, and it was marked for identification.

"What kind of truck were you driving? Was this a company truck?"

"A pickup. It's my own vehicle, a Ford F-150."

I remembered the big white truck that had pulled in behind us as we pulled away from the pumps. I didn't like the way this was developing. When you're going to have to do your best to discredit a witness, it's nice not to know he's telling the truth.

"Could you tell us about the person who was in the vehicle just ahead of yours?"

"There at the pumps? The only one I saw was a tall woman with straight blonde hair. She got into the passenger side of the car, and it pulled away."

"So there was more than one person in the car?"

"I assume so. Somebody would have had to be behind the wheel."

"But you just saw the woman with straight blonde hair."

"That's right. She threw something into the trash can and got in the car."

"That's the trash can at the pump island?"

"Yes."

"The pump island where pump number eight is located?"

He nodded. "That's the pump on my receipt."

"And this woman was at the same pump island where you got your gas?"

"She was."

"Did you ever see this woman again? This tall woman with the straight blonde hair?" If there was a less attractive-sounding description of a woman, I couldn't think what it was.

"I did," Jeffries said.

"Where?"

"I picked her out of a lineup at the police station on Grace Street."

"Who was she?"

He glanced at me, then away. He took a breath. "Robin Starling."

"Who?"

"Robin Starling, the attorney right over there." He pointed.

"The attorney for the defense was in this lineup?" Biggs' incredulity was way overdone, I thought, given the build-up.

I half-stood behind my table. "Asked and answered."

Judge Cheatham frowned at me.

"Never mind," Biggs said. "Those are all my questions." He gathered up his papers and gave me a smile as he tapped them on the podium to straighten them. His expression was triumphant.

I went to the podium, laid down my legal pad and straightened it. I laid my pen beside it, perfectly parallel to the long edge. It was time for me to do my magic, and my bag of tricks was pretty empty. I looked up at the witness.

"You said you saw this woman throw something away," I said.

He nodded. "That's right."

"You didn't say what."

"I didn't see."

"Didn't see sunlight flashing off a chrome surface?"

"No."

"A glint of blued steel?" The gun I'd thrown in the trashcan didn't meet either of those descriptions, and I'd carried it in a wad of blue paper towels, so the questions seemed pretty safe.

"No. I didn't see anything."

"So she could have thrown away a candy wrapper, as far as you know?'

"She could have."

"Or something as small as a piece of gum."

"I didn't see what she threw away."

"Detective McClane testified that at the time of the lineup, you were 'pretty sure' about your identification of the woman you saw."

"I was."

"Are those the words you used? 'Pretty sure'?"

"I think so. It sounds about right."

"So he didn't say, 'How sure are you?' And you didn't respond, 'Absolutely sure.' Or 'positive,' or some other expression to that effect?"

"I guess not."

"Because you weren't absolutely sure, were you?"

He shifted in his seat, cleared his throat. "I guess I wasn't absolutely sure at the time. When I thought about it, though…"

"Did you acquire some new data to inform your thinking?" I said, interrupting.

"No. I just thought about it."

"You remembered the woman from the gas station, and you compared that memory to the

213

memory of the woman you'd seen in the lineup, and both memories became sharper over time?"

"It wasn't just memory. I looked you up on the internet."

"Ah. And as you stared at my face it began to seem more and more familiar?"

"I guess it did."

If I didn't know that R was the woman he'd seen, I'd have no confidence at all in his identification, I thought. "Detective McClane said he thought he probably warned you that the woman you'd seen at the gas station might not be in the lineup. Given his use of not one but two qualifiers, 'probably' and 'might not,' I'll ask you: Did he give you that warning?"

"I don't know. I don't remember it."

"So as you studied the lineup, you weren't thinking, the woman I saw might not be here."

"No. I wasn't."

"You were expecting to see her."

"I was."

"And because you were expecting to see her, you picked out the woman whose appearance most resembled the woman you'd seen."

"Sure."

I looked at Biggs. "Your witness."

He came to the podium for redirect. He said, "The fact is that you remembered seeing a tall blonde woman at the gas station, and, when you were presented with a lineup of six women roughly matching that description, you picked out Ms. Starling."

I was at the defense table, but hadn't yet taken my seat. "Objection," I said. "Leading."

"Did you identify Ms. Starling, or didn't you?" Biggs said.

"I guess I did."

"You guess you did?" Biggs said, his voice rising in pitch. "You're saying that right now you don't know if you identified Ms. Starling?"

"No. I did identify her."

"Thank you." Biggs left the podium and walked jerkily back to his seat.

When court recessed for the day, Willow said, "Are you going to be in trouble over that identification?"

I nodded, shrugged. "Maybe. Actually, I wouldn't be surprised if I was charged as an accessory after the fact. On the other hand, if Mr. Jeffries is no more certain than he was today, a good attorney ought to be able to raise a reasonable doubt."

"And you're a good attorney," Willow said.

"I'm beginning to wonder. If I was charged with a felony, I don't think I'd represent myself. 'An attorney who represents himself has a fool for a client.' That's what they say anyway."

So I might represent myself, if it came to it.

Chapter 11

Aubrey Biggs was not quite done, evidently. When court recessed, he'd gone to the judge's bench. Now Judge Cheatham called, "Ms. Starling?"

I went forward.

Biggs said, "Your honor, I need to call your attention to an abuse of process being perpetrated by defense counsel."

I couldn't help it. I rolled my eyes.

Judge Cheatham said, "This is a serious matter, Ms. Starling."

"I'm sorry, your honor. He's just presented some very suspect eye-witness testimony to the effect that I disposed of a murder weapon. Now it's abuse of process. I can't even imagine what he's talking about, but somehow it all seems a bit much."

"It is nevertheless a serious matter."

"Yes, your honor. I'm sorry."

"Mr. Biggs?"

He turned his head to scan the gallery, now almost empty of spectators. "Peyton Shilling? Will you stand?"

She alone was still in her seat. She stood and came to the rail. She was wearing a plaid skirt, a white blouse, and a thin blue sweater. Her hair was in braids. I couldn't see her feet, so maybe she wasn't wearing saddle oxfords to complete the school-girl image. Actually, given her chest and hips and her narrow waist, she looked more like a stripper dressed as a school girl for the beginning of her act. Given that we were dealing with a couple of men here, she'd probably managed just the right look.

"Your honor," Biggs said. "Ms. Starling has served a subpoena on this young woman for no purpose other than to intimidate and humiliate her. Her presence in court today has served no purpose, and her presence tomorrow will serve no purpose."

Judge Cheatham said, "Ms. Starling?"

"Your honor, if Mr. Biggs had finished his case and allowed me to begin mine, I might well have gotten to call Ms. Shilling. Instead, he's gone off down a rabbit hole on a matter that has nothing to do with the guilt or innocence of this defendant, but is motivated entirely by his personal animus toward me."

Cheatham's gaze shifted to Aubrey Biggs, whose nostrils had begun flaring with each intake of breath. He was personal animus personified.

He said, "Perhaps Ms. Starling doesn't think accessory-after-the-fact is a serious charge—"

"Oh, I think it's very serious. That's why its introduction here is so prejudicial to the rights of the defendant. It's one effort he's made to intimidate defense counsel. This abuse-of-process charge is another."

"That's ridiculous."

"That isn't a denial, is it, Aubrey?"

The judge said, "That's enough. Ms. Starling, do you intend to call Ms. Shilling as part of your case?"

"I do, your honor."

"This is a preliminary hearing. Counsel doesn't intend to present a case at all," Biggs said.

"You're telling me that you do plan to present evidence on the defendant's behalf," Judge Cheatham said to me.

"I do, your honor."

"And you intend to call Ms. Shilling as part of your case."

Biggs said, "I have questioned Ms. Shilling myself. She is in possession of no facts that would be helpful to the defense."

"Mr. Biggs is being disingenuous at best, if not outright misleading," I said. "He intends to call her as part of his case at trial, and this objection is part of a continuing effort to deny me the opportunity to question her."

Biggs said, "Just because the decedent abused his position as a college instructor to seduce this young woman—"

"Seduce *her!*"

"Yes, seduce her, and possibly even force her."

"Your honor, this Peyton Shilling has the prosecutor so bamboozled he doesn't recognize motive when it's been gift-wrapped for him and tied with a ribbon."

Judge Cheatham said, "If she supplies a motive for your client, I don't see that her testimony is relevant to your defense. A preliminary hearing is not a discovery tool. It's to make sure the commonwealth has probable cause to hold the defendant for trial."

"Your honor. Motive is a sword that cuts both ways. Peyton Shilling is the other woman. She's the third side of the triangle." I tried to think of another cliché and couldn't. "At the time of his death, she was actually a student of Chris Woodruff at J. Sargent Reynolds, a student who was having an affair with her instructor. The decedent was living with her for a good part of this past academic year."

Biggs said, "The seduction of this girl occurred months before the decedent's death. Mr. Woodruff had returned home to his wife. Ms. Shilling had returned to her studies. There was an end to it."

Cheatham's gaze rose to the school girl standing at the rail, then returned to me.

"Ms. Starling? What facts precisely do you expect to prove with this witness?"

"I can't tell you precisely, your honor. She has refused to talk to me, but I believe her to be in possession of important facts. This isn't the way I would prefer to get at them. Because of her lack of cooperation, I have been forced to issue a subpoena to bring her into court to answer questions under oath."

"To go poking through her personal life in a public forum is what you mean," Biggs said. "Your honor, I move that this subpoena be quashed. Peyton Shilling is a victim, and putting her on the stand will only victimize her further."

"The prosecutor is certain to call her as his own witness at trial. If you quash this subpoena, the defendant will be unable to get at exculpatory facts that are known to this witness. It will seriously compromise this defendant's ability to prepare and to present her case," I said.

Judge Cheatham looked at Biggs. "Under the circumstances I have no choice but to let the subpoena stand."

"If Ms. Starling fails to elicit relevant testimony, I will be asking this court for sanctions against her."

"Your honor, I hesitate to keep pointing out the obvious, but once again Mr. Biggs is using his office in an attempt to intimidate counsel."

"And when counsel puts this young woman on the stand," Biggs said. "*If* she puts her on the stand, I will be objecting to every question on the grounds of relevance."

Judge Cheatham said to me, "You do understand that this court will be unforgiving if it turns out you have no reason for calling this witness other than purposes of harassment and delay."

"If fulfilling my duty to my client requires me to operate under the threat of sanctions, so be it," I said.

The judge's head went back, and his expression darkened. "I think that statement betrays an unfortunate attitude on your part, Ms. Starling."

"Me, too," I said.

Biggs went to the rail to console little Miss Muffet. I'd once heard him described as very married, and, under these circumstances, he probably needed to be. I pushed past them through the bar and went down the aisle. To cap a perfect day in court, Carter Fox was waiting for me in an aisle seat on the last row.

I slowed as I noticed him, and he stood. "Do you have your car here, or may I give you a ride back to the office?" he said.

I looked at my watch. I'd walked across downtown that morning as I always did. This evening I needed the walk back to fume and to clear my head.

"Come on. I've got a space right on the curb," he said.

I sighed. "All right. Thank you."

"The Carter Fox Executive Limousine Service is at your disposal." He cackled and rubbed his hands.

There were half-a-dozen other people waiting for the elevator. On the ride down with them, Carter said, "You were great in there today, as always." Crowded against me, he seemed to be addressing these remarks to my breasts, blinking owlishly at them through his thick lenses.

I felt my lip curl. "So what do you think?" I said to the top of his head. "Was I the woman Colton Jeffries saw at the gas station, or wasn't I?" All conversation stopped, and everybody looked at me, which suggested that some or all of them had been in the courtroom.

"Ha! I couldn't say, I really couldn't. You'd know better than anybody."

"Knowing I'm innocent and convincing a jury are two different things." I raised my voice slightly. "How many of you were in the courtroom just now?"

It seemed that everybody was.

"Who thinks Colton Jeffries was correct in identifying me as the woman he saw at the Valero station?"

An elderly man with his pants belted over his paunch raised his hand. Several other hands followed. It looked unanimous.

"Anyone think he might have made a mistake?"

A girl I hadn't noticed before raised a hand. She had long, mousy brown hair and was wearing glasses with large, round lenses.

I gave her a smile as the elevator doors opened and people started getting out. "So what causes you to give me the benefit of the doubt?"

"Body language."

"Mine or the witness's?"

"The witness's. I can't read you at all, but I think Mr. Jeffries is very uncertain at this point that he knows who he saw. He's caught now, though, and doesn't know how to get out of it."

"Well, that's a hopeful thought."

"You're good," she said. "I've gotten a lot out of watching you."

Conscious of Carter Fox hovering just within earshot, I said, "What do you do for a living, if you don't mind my asking?"

"Oh, I don't mind. I'm a theatre performance major at VCU."

"And you're in court today because…"

"I've been cast as a lawyer in VCU's production of *Night of January 16*, Ayn Rand's play. I've gotten some super pointers, I think. You've got some great mannerisms I can use."

"Thanks, I guess."

"Oh, I mean it as a compliment. I've got class in the morning, or I'd be back. I'd love to see how this turns out."

On foot, the trip from the courthouse to my office takes about fifteen minutes. In Carter Fox's aging Corvette with the broken door handle—I didn't ask—the trip was interminable. He wanted to talk about the trial, and I wanted to talk about anything but. Actually, I didn't want to talk at all, but that didn't seem to be an option.

"So where do you see the case going next?" he asked me.

"Hard to say."

"The D.A. seems to be focusing more on you than on the defendant at this point, don't you think?"

"It seems that way."

"So how's it going to turn out? Do you think you're going to be in trouble with the state bar?"

"I can hope not."

"Surely you have a plan."

"I do have a plan, but my name's not Shirley."

He laughed, too loudly, his head bobbing genially behind the wheel. I winced. There was still one person in the world who thought I was funny, but somehow I wasn't encouraged.

The conversation went on. It was the verbal equivalent of Chinese water torture. Was I really going to present evidence? Did I think my client might actually be innocent? Surely I wasn't going to put her on the stand. "There I go calling you Shirley again," he said, and honked with laughter. After a day or a day-and-a-half, he pulled up in front of the Ironfronts. I looked at my watch and saw that the ride had actually taken ten minutes. I wouldn't have held out long against the Chinese.

"It's too close to five o'clock for me to park on the street," Carter said, and my spirits lifted. Cars got towed after five, a bit of heavy-handed law enforcement I had never appreciated until that moment. "I'll just let you off and head on back to the ranch."

I got out of his car. "Get along, little dogie," I said, and closed the door on his honk of laughter. He pulled away, and I turned into the Ironfronts.

Rodney Burns came out of his office as I was unlocking mine. "I got what you asked for," he said.

For a moment I stared at him blankly, then I remembered. "South of Main Limited," I said. "You got the filings. Give me a minute, and I'll come to your office."

But he was back in my doorway almost immediately. I dropped into my chair. "What you got?" I said.

He put a folder in front of me. "Something that will surprise you, I think. At any rate it surprised me."

I opened the folder, conscious of him watching me. On top was the Certificate of Limited Partnership, which I'd seen online. Peyton Shilling was the registered agent, and the general partner was CF Development, Inc. The signature of the person who'd signed for the corporation was completely illegible, a single wiggly line with a spike in the middle. It struck me that the name should be printed underneath the signature line, but it wasn't there. I turned the page.

The second document was CF Development's Certificate of Incorporation. The registered agent again was Peyton Shilling, no real surprise, but the shocker came at the end. The signature of the incorporator was the same wiggly line with the spike, and this time the name was printed underneath: Carter Fox.

"Holy moley," I said.

"Is it anything you can use?"

"I don't know. It's got to be." I looked up from the documents. "Thanks, Rodney. You've done wonders."

I found Carly Price in the copy room. The copier was churning out a gazillion copies of something or other, and Carly was using a long stapler to make pamphlets out of the stack of offset copies that were already sitting on the work table.

"You're in the middle of something," I said.

"Whatcha need?"

"I don't want to interrupt."

She put down the stapler and tucked some errant strands of curly hair behind her ear to get them out of her face. "Anything for my favorite tenant." She gestured with her head at the stacks of paper beside her. "Besides, this is a nightmare. I'd be happy to wake from it."

"Actually, I'm glad to hear you say that about me being your favorite tenant. I need you to play favorites."

She searched my face with enormous brown eyes. "Okay."

"I need to search Carter Fox's office."

"Oh, my."

"I know. I'm asking you to violate a trust. You can tell me no if you need to. I just don't know what I'm going to do if you do." My mouth stretched in a quick grimace.

After a moment's indecision, she stood. "I've had to give up all my low-cut blouses since he moved in. Have you noticed? When I show just a little bit of cleavage, he looks like he's going to put his nose in it."

I laughed and felt immediately better. I hadn't realized what a strain I was under.

"Let me get my keys," she said.

She unlocked the door and removed her keys. "I'll stand guard in the hall."

"Okay," I said. "If you see him, hoot twice like a barn owl."

"Like a what?"

"Never mind. Sorry."

"Can't I just whisper he's coming?"

"That will be fine.

Carter Fox had a smaller office than I did, only about eight or ten feet square, most of the space taken up by a desk and two client chairs pushed against the wall. There was not even a desktop computer, though I thought he might carry a laptop around in that briefcase of his. I slid into the office chair and started opening drawers.

There was surprisingly little there. I knew Carter was a lawyer; the law license hanging on his wall was testament to that, but there was no filing cabinet in the office and just a single unlabeled file in one of the desk drawers.

"You don't store files for him anywhere, do you?" I called as I took out the folder and laid it on the desk.

Carly appeared in the doorway. "No. Can you keep it down? Not everyone's gone home yet."

"Sorry." I opened the folder, and my picture stared up at me. It was part of a newspaper article that had appeared during my last trial. I shifted it to one side and saw another article beneath it, also about me.

Carly, who had caught sight of the photograph, leaned over the desk. "It's like he's stalking you."

"My number one fan," I said.

There were more articles, six in all, and there were more photographs printed out on copy paper. I had no idea when they were taken. In one I was standing in front of the courthouse. In another, I was wearing a blouse I had taken to Goodwill a couple of months ago. In the last one, I was sitting on the front stoop of my house with my chin in my hands, probably waiting for Deacon to do his business.

"I think he's fixated on you."

I shivered as a gaggle of geese paraded across my gravesite. I looked up blindly. "Aren't you standing guard?" I said.

"Oh, right." She disappeared again into the hallway, pulling the door almost shut as she went.

I gave myself a shake and went back to work. Carter had office supplies in his desk—pens, legal pads, paper clips, folders—but the legal pads were blank. There was no evidence of work in progress anywhere. What did he do when he was in his office, other than sit and look at pictures of me?

I pulled the middle drawer out all the way and reached in for the small manila envelope at the back. It was only about the size of a credit card. I opened the flap and spilled two keys into my palm. One of them had the distinctive diamond-shaped bow of the office keys at the Ironfronts. The other looked a lot like my house key.

The implications dizzied me. The day when I couldn't find my keys had been the very day that Brooke and I met Carter Fox. Had I left my keys on my desk, and had Carter found a moment that morning when he could walk into my office and out again unseen? After that one act of daring, everything would have been easy—getting copies made of my office and house keys, returning everything to the kitchen on the far side of the coffee maker. I shook my head, thinking. I'd had my locks changed. There was no way to verify my suspicions or to discredit them. The main thing for now was not to alert Carter Fox and put him on his guard. I put the keys back in the envelope and pushed it to the back of the drawer.

When I'd gotten my breathing under control, I stepped out and closed the office door behind me. Carly exhaled noisily. "Thank goodness," she said. "I kept expecting him to turn into the hall at any minute. I don't know what I would have done."

"You need to learn how to hoot like a barn owl."

She gave me a look, and I smiled, though I still felt sick.

"What did you find?" she asked me. "Anything else?"

"I don't know. Maybe the keys to my home and office."

Her eyes grew wide. "Robin! That man is dangerous."

"I think he may be."

"What are you going to do?" She stepped closer. "I worry about you, you know. You don't know how to be careful."

I put an arm around her and patted her back to comfort her. Somehow, it made me feel better, too.

Chapter 12

When I entered the courtroom the next morning, I was armed with a subpoena for Carter Fox, which I carried in one hand with my briefcase in the other. My plan was to serve the subpoena as I entered the courtroom, but Carter, who had been in the courtroom every day of the trial so far, wasn't there. Brooke was, though, with a seat on the aisle. I leaned over her.

"Have you seen Carter Fox this morning?"

"No, thank goodness."

"Watch for him, will you? And if you see him, give him this." I handed her the subpoena. "My plan is to put him on the stand and tickle his tonsils a little."

She made a face. "You're going to make out with Carter Fox in the courtroom?"

I straightened. "You've got a one-track mind," I said.

There were nearly a dozen people in the gallery, among them Peyton Shilling, but no one was on the other side of the railing yet. I pushed through the bar and sat alone at the defense table. Maybe *tickle his*

229

tonsils wasn't the best metaphor for a grueling examination. Though I'd majored in English in college, none of my professors had ever mistaken me for a poet.

James Jordan and Ray Hernandez came in and sat on the first row of the gallery, directly behind me. I gave them a sharp look, but Hernandez only gave me a finger wave.

I leaned over the bar. "What are you doing here? This isn't your case."

"We're here to arrest you," Jordan said, "unless you can pull off another one of your Houdini tricks."

"Arrest me in the middle of the preliminary? You're kidding."

"We'll wait until it's over. Our instructions are to arrest you and charge you as an accessory after the fact just as soon as the judge binds the defendant over for trial."

"That's not nice."

"We're cops," Hernandez said. "Nobody expects us to be nice."

"Well you could look more broken up about it. And you're likely to be here all day, you know."

"Aubrey doesn't think so."

Speak of the devil. I turned away from them as Aubrey Biggs came in and thumped his briefcase down on the other table. He gave me a curt nod. "Ms. Starling."

"Mr. Biggs." I always felt like I was talking to a cartoon character when I called him that, but I needed to take him seriously. I looked back over the gallery, past Jordan and Hernandez, but Carter Fox still wasn't there. Brooke had moved over a seat, though, leaving an empty one on the aisle—an invitation for Carter Fox to sit beside her if ever there was one. I gave her a nod of approval.

As soon as Willow Woodruff had been ushered in, the bailiff called the court into session with his "Oyez, oyez," and Judge Cheatham came in and took a seat. We all sat after him.

"We're here in the case of Commonwealth versus Woodruff. Mr. Biggs, call your next witness."

"The prosecution rests, your honor."

It was a surprise, but perhaps it shouldn't have been. All Biggs had to show was that a crime had been committed—not a big stretch when a man's found lying on his bed with his brains blown out—and that there was probable cause to believe the defendant committed it. The standard of proof is much lower than at trial, where the prosecutor has to prove each element of the crime beyond a reasonable doubt. If Biggs hadn't been after me as much as he was Willow Woodruff, he'd have probably rested before now.

The judge looked at me. "Will there be a defense?"

The smart answer here is usually no. Why give the prosecution a chance to test your case before you are playing for real stakes before a jury? I glanced back into the gallery. Still no Carter Fox, just Peyton Shilling, meeting my gaze defiantly. If I wanted to question her under oath, this was my chance.

"Yes, your honor."

"You really have exculpatory evidence that you think has a chance of clearing your client?"

"Maybe."

The judge looked resigned. "Very well. Go ahead with your opening statement."

"I'd rather begin with my first witness."

231

He cut his eyes toward the ceiling and waved a hand.

Once again I looked out over the gallery. Was Carter Fox just busy on other matters, or had he somehow become aware that I was onto him? I didn't see how he could have, but there might be some bizarre combination of coincidences that accounted for it.

"Ms. Starling?"

"Call Peyton Shilling," I said.

Peyton came forward. Yesterday she'd looked like a schoolgirl. Today she looked like fashion model. Her unbound hair flowed past her shoulders, and she was wearing a simple shift dress with three-quarter sleeves. The light brown fabric with its slightly darker geometric pattern brought out her dark eyes and the honey tones in her skin. I wondered if the change in appearance represented a change in tactics on her part.

She was sworn in and took her seat in the witness box, giving her skirt a pointless tug in the direction of her knees. Judge Cheatham, I noted, seemed to be taking full advantage of his elevated vantage point.

Biggs was on his feet behind his table. "Your honor, I object to the calling of this witness. Counsel's calling her is an abuse of process, and at the conclusion of her testimony I will be asking this court to impose sanctions."

"Ms. Starling?"

"Oh, come on."

"Pardon?"

I heaved a big sigh. "Your honor, what Mr. Biggs really objects to is a vigorous defense and my zealous representation of my client. He has two police officers sitting immediately behind me to let me know I'm going to be arrested at the conclusion of this hearing. He has threatened me with prosecution, and now he is threatening me with sanctions. He's a big bully who lacks any confidence in the strength of his case against Willow Woodruff. All he has are scare tactics and intimidation, tools that are available to him only because of his office and his willingness to abuse it."

I glanced at Biggs and was pleased to see his face reddening.

He said, "Your honor, those statements are defamatory, and I demand that Ms. Starling retract them."

The one thing I wasn't worried about was a suit for defamation. Statements made in judicial proceedings are protected by an absolute privilege, a privilege Mr. Biggs himself had been taking advantage of.

"Is the defendant entitled to call witnesses in her defense, or isn't she?" I asked.

"She is. Of course she is." The judge looked down into the lap of this particular witness, nodding his head judiciously.

"This witness has nothing to say helpful for the defense," Biggs said.

"I believe she does, though Mr. Biggs may be in a better position to know than I am. She certainly seems to have given him the curtesy of an interview as well as a good look at her long, silky legs."

Judge Cheatham jerked his gaze away from what might have been his view of those very legs.

Biggs said, "Perhaps the witness objects to your pointless snooping into the private details of her personal life."

"Perhaps she does."

He took a breath. "So you agree not to call her?"

"No. Perhaps I don't give a damn. I've called Peyton Shilling, and I intend to question her."

To the judge Biggs said, "And I intend to object to every question that is not strictly relevant to this case." To me: "We'll see how far you get."

Cheatham rapped his gavel. "That's enough, Mr. Biggs. You can make your objections at the appropriate time."

"Thank you, your honor," I said. "Ms. Shilling. Could you tell us your full name, please?"

It was Peyton Quincy Shilling. I got her address into the record, and her occupation as a yoga instructor. So far, no objections.

"Are you also a student at J Sargent Reynolds?" Still no objection.

"Yes. I take a course or two every semester."

"Is that where you met Christopher Woodruff?"

"Objection," Biggs said.

"Overruled."

With the judge's quick ruling, I bit back my own response. "Answer the question," I said.

"Yes, that's where I met him."

"He was a professor in one of the classes you were taking?"

"Objection. Relevance."

"Overruled."

Biggs face was turning red again, and I smiled—but only on the inside.

"I had him for microeconomics," Peyton said.

234

"Was fall of last year the first semester you'd had him?"

"No, I had him for personal finance the semester before that."

"What was your relationship with Chris Woodruff, other than student-teacher?"

"I really must object," Biggs said. "This can have no purpose but to smear the reputation of this young woman."

"Ms. Starling?"

"Any innuendo is coming from the prosecutor, your honor—though really, if she didn't have any kind of relationship with the decedent or the defendant, there would be no point in my calling her."

"My point exactly," Biggs said.

"But you did have a relationship with Chris Woodruff, didn't you, Ms. Shilling?"

"We were friends."

"Don't answer her questions!" Biggs said. "Don't answer until the judge has a chance to rule on my objections."

"Friends with benefits?" I said.

"You see, your honor? There it is. That's what I was talking about."

Judge Cheatham said, "Just where are you going with this, Ms. Starling? Are you proposing a motive for this witness?"

"I am. I believe I can establish that Chris Woodruff left his wife and moved in with this witness," I said. "That he purchased two identical handguns and gave the one registered in his wife's name to Ms. Shilling for her protection." Biggs was shouting, and I had to raise my voice to be heard over his shrill objections. "That Ms. Shilling was bitter when he left her and moved back in…"

I had to give up. Biggs was shouting and waving his arms and all but dancing behind his table. "Objection! There is no basis for any of these remarks. They are defamatory and inflammatory and highly prejudicial, and I most strenuously object. I—"

"The judge asked me what I hoped to prove," I shouted back at him. "I was telling him."

"You might hope to prove that Istanbul is the capital of France! That doesn't mean you have any basis for such a statement."

The judge banged his gavel.

"We might see what kind of basis there was if the witness were allowed to answer questions," I said.

"Ms. Starling!" Judge Cheatham whacked his gavel on the bench again.

"I'm sorry, your honor."

He turned to Peyton Shilling. "Did Christopher Woodruff ever give you a handgun?" he asked.

"He certainly did not." She said it with conviction. If she was a liar, she was a good liar.

"You're aware you're under oath, that any falsehoods would make you liable to prosecution for perjury?" the judge said.

"Yes, your honor."

"In light of that answer, I'm not going to allow any more questions about this witness's relationship with the decedent. Not until something more has been laid by way of foundation."

It was a blow. "Very well, your honor."

"Do you have any more questions of this witness?"

"A few. Ms. Shilling…"

She looked at me in wide-eyed innocence.

"What is your relationship with a lawyer named Carter Fox?"

She flinched, and I saw it. The clamor that sprang up at once from the prosecution's table, whatever the judge was saying, all of it faded to background noise.

Her eyes had widened, and her mouth was pursed as if she were saying, "Who?" beneath the hubbub.

"With Carter Fox," I said, more loudly. "The lawyer who sold Chris Woodruff one-and-a-half shares in a limited partnership called South of Main for a grand total of sixty thousand dollars."

"What makes you think I..."

Biggs was saying something, so I increased my volume another notch to override him. "You also have an interest in that partnership, don't you? Now what is your connection to Carter Fox?"

"He's my brother." It was almost a whisper. I glanced at the court reporter to make sure he'd caught it.

"He's your brother," I repeated.

"My half-brother."

Biggs, at last, fell silent. The entire courtroom seemed to ring with silence.

"Is Carter Fox the sole owner of CF Development, Incorporated, or do you also have an interest?"

She hesitated, her mouth open, but no sound coming out.

I said, "It's a matter of public record, you know."

"I have a share. That's all. Just the one share."

"CF Development is the general partner in South of Main Limited?"

She nodded.

"Yes?" I said.

"Yes."

"And what does South of Main do?"

"Pardon?"

"South of Main buys and sells real estate, and it manages rental properties, doesn't it?"

She looked past me into the gallery, and I turned to follow her gaze. If she was looking for Carter Fox, he wasn't there.

Biggs stood up. "Your honor, the relevance of all this is not clear to me, and in any case counsel is leading the witness."

"Rephrase your question," Judge Cheatham told me.

"I'll leave that question and go to the next one, your honor." To Peyton I said, "How did you talk Chris Woodruff into investing in South of Main? Did you and he buy that first share together?"

Again she nodded.

"Out loud, Ms. Shilling. Did you buy a share together?"

"Yes."

"His half of the share cost twenty thousand dollars. How much did yours cost? How much will your bank records showed you paid for your half?"

She shook her head.

"You didn't pay anything, did you? Your contribution was finding Chris Woodruff and reeling him in."

"It wasn't like that. I thought it was a good investment, so I told Chris about it. Mr. Woodruff."

"But you didn't put your own money into it, did you? Did you, Ms. Shilling?"

"I didn't have any to put."

"No," I agreed. "What you had was youth and beauty."

I went back to the defense table to get the South of Main brochure, gave a photocopy of it to Aubrey Biggs, and took the original to the judge. "I'd like to show this to the witness."

Judge Cheatham nodded.

"Ms. Shilling, have you ever seen this brochure before?"

"Sure. I've seen it."

"Are you aware that of all the properties pictured here South of Main owns only one?"

She stared at me.

"It's never owned any of the others. Are you aware of that?"

"No."

"So what you did was perpetrate a fraud on Chris Woodruff, you and your brother. For sixty thousand dollars you sold him shares in a limited partnership that didn't own the assets it purported to own."

"I didn't know."

"In Chris Woodruff's file cabinet I found copies of the most recent deeds to four of these properties that are pictured in the brochure, but which are not owned by South of Main and never have been. That means that Chris Woodruff found out about the fraud, didn't he? Is that when he left you?"

She shook her head. "He didn't...We just..."

"He left you and demanded the return of his money. He never got it, though, did he? Before he could take things further, he was shot through the head in his own house. Was it you who shot him, or was it your brother Carter Fox?"

"I didn't shoot him. Neither of us did."

"He was found in his boxer shorts. Chris might have let you into the house without his pants on, but he'd have hardly let in your brother."

"I didn't do it."

"Did Carter Fox?"

"I don't know. How could I know?"

"You testified that neither of you shot Chris Woodruff. Do you now wish to change your answer from 'neither of us did' to 'I don't know'?"

"No, I…"

"Did you have a key to the Woodruff residence?"

"No."

"Did Chris Woodruff give you the key, or did you get hold of his keys at some point during your relationship and secretly make a copy of his house key?"

"No."

"And did you give that copy of the key to your brother?"

She came out of her seat in the witness box. "No!" she shouted at me. "No to all of it. I never had a key. I didn't do anything wrong." She looked at Aubrey Biggs, then up at the judge. Her face crumpled suddenly, and she sank back into her chair as she began to cry.

I waited. The court waited. Even Biggs remained silent. "I didn't do anything wrong," she said finally. She lifted her head then and sniffed, her face wet with tears. "And I'm done answering your questions. I'm not going to say another word until I can talk to my lawyer."

Judge Cheatham leaned over her. "Are you saying that answering further questions may tend to incriminate you?" he asked. "Are you asserting your Fifth Amendment privilege?"

"I am."

Chapter 13

Peyton Shilling left the stand. She pushed through the rail and walked straight down the aisle and out of the courtroom. Brooke stood, her eyebrows raised, but I shook my head. Peyton Shilling was an athletic woman with a predilection for kicking people. Following her didn't make sense from a risk-reward standpoint.

"Your next witness, Ms. Starling."

"Your honor, I've prepared a subpoena commanding the appearance of Carter Fox, but so far I have been unable to serve it on him. I request a continuance to give me time to do so."

Biggs, predictably, objected. "Carter Fox is not on her witness list, your honor. This is the time and place set for this hearing, and counsel has had ample time to prepare her case."

"I'm inclined to agree with the prosecutor, Ms. Starling."

"I'd been looking into the withdrawals of sixty thousand dollars from the decedent's brokerage and retirement accounts, your honor, and the checks written to South of Main. I'd become aware that the partnership didn't seem to own the property listed in its brochures, but I didn't find out about Carter Fox's connection to the partnership until late yesterday."

"When did you become aware that he was related to Peyton Shilling?"

"This morning when I got her on the stand. I'd known Peyton was connected to South of Main. I didn't know about Mr. Fox's connection to it until after court yesterday. The brother-sister thing took me completely by surprise."

"Your honor," Biggs said. "What possible difference does it make who she's related to? None of us ever heard of Carter Fox before this morning."

"We've heard evidence this morning that Carter Fox defrauded Chris Woodruff of sixty thousand dollars."

"No, we didn't. We've heard your allegations to that effect."

The judge banged his gavel. "Please address your remarks to the court," he said.

Biggs said, "Your honor, even if she can show that South of Main doesn't own the property pictured in that brochure, it doesn't make any difference to the disposition of this case. After all, this is a preliminary hearing. Yes, maybe there was some kind of connection between the decedent and this Carter Fox. So what? So she speculates that the decedent was about to expose the man. That maybe it gave him a motive for murder, but what we've heard so far is that he had no opportunity. The defendant's own witness has denied that either he or she had access to the murder weapon or to the house."

"That's why I need to get him on the stand," I said. "Counsel can hardly complain that my evidence is insufficient, then deny me the opportunity to produce more."

"You think you're going to put him on the stand, and he's just going to admit to everything you accuse him of?"

The judge tapped his gavel as a reminder for Biggs to make his arguments to the court.

"Sorry, your honor," he said, "but this is a fantasy. At a preliminary hearing, the commonwealth has to show that a murder has been committed and that there's probable cause to think that this defendant was responsible. We've done that. Christopher Woodruff died in his own bed of a gunshot wound. Trace amounts of gunshot residue was found on the defendant's hands. The murder weapon came into the possession of defense counsel, who disposed of it in a gas station trashcan. If Christopher Woodruff had been having an affair, as counsel alleges, we have motive. What counsel proposes is that we stretch out this proceeding for no purpose other than for her to present conflicting evidence, which would be appropriate at trial, but not here. Conflicting evidence is a matter for a jury."

As a closing argument, it was a pretty good one, though he hadn't actually introduced evidence of the gunshot residue: All McClane had told us was that Willow had been tested for it. Judge Cheatham looked at me for a response.

"Your honor, there's a reason we need to pursue this now. The district attorney has placed two police detectives directly behind me with instructions to arrest me as an accessory after the fact as soon as this hearing is concluded. It is at best disingenuous for him to deny me the opportunity to develop evidence here in this courtroom when he intends to deny me the opportunity to develop it afterwards."

"Mr. Biggs?"

"That's not my problem, your honor. You heard the evidence against her. An eyewitness picked her out of a lineup as the woman he saw throw something in the trashcan where the murder weapon was found."

"I heard the testimony. I agree it casts counsel in an unfortunate light." He gave me a disapproving glance. "It was hardly conclusive, though. Can't you pursue your cases one at a time? Present your evidence again at trial, and if it holds up, bring your charges against Ms. Starling at that time?"

"I don't feel I can, your honor. The demands of justice require us to hold her to account for her actions."

"Justice delayed is justice denied?"

"Exactly, your honor."

He had picked up his gavel. "Very well. Ms. Starling, I'm going to grant you your continuance."

Biggs threw out a hand. "Wait, your honor."

The judge waited, his eyebrows elevated.

Biggs swallowed. "Suppose we charge her, but agree to release her on her own recognizance? She'll be free to develop any evidence she wants."

The judge shook his head. "This is a serious matter, Mr. Biggs. I'm not going to force counsel to operate under that kind of cloud if things can be cleared up in this courtroom. How much time do you need, Ms. Starling?"

I asked for a week. I got until the following Monday. Biggs gathered up his things and stuffed them violently into his briefcase. His hand on the handle, he gave me a dark look.

"See you Monday," I said.

"You can't dodge this forever. We'll get you."

I gave him a smile.

Willow was looking at me with what seemed to be an anxious expression. "Are trials always like this?"

I shook my head. "I just have a knack for pissing off the prosecutor."

She leaned toward me so that our heads were touching. "Did you do it?" she asked. "Throw the gun away like they said?"

I patted her hand, smiled. "That would be a crime," I said.

She took that as a no, but of course it wasn't a denial.

Jordan and Hernandez followed Brooke and me out of the courtroom. I glanced around at them as I went through the tall double doors, but didn't say anything until we were on the elevator and it was just us.

"To what do I owe the pleasure?" I said.

"The pleasure's ours," Jordan said. "We have a couple of hours free that we'd expected to spend booking you and searching you…"

"Having a female officer search you, actually," Hernandez said. "Protocol frowns on us doing anything we might enjoy."

"…fingerprinting you and taking your mug shots," Jordan continued.

"Always following the proprieties, of course," Hernandez said.

246

"I would expect nothing less," I said.

"So, are you going to slip the noose again this time, do you think?"

"It'll be a near thing."

"We have confidence in you," Jordan said, and I gave him a sour smile as the doors slid open on the ground floor.

"There is something you could do for me, actually," I said.

"What is it?"

"We're always at the service of the defense bar," Hernandez said.

"That may be overstating it," Jordan said.

They nodded to the security guard, and we pushed out through the revolving door. Already it was turning into a hot, muggy day. We stopped, blinking in the morning sun. "Do you need a ride back to the office?" Brooke asked me.

"We've got her covered," Jordan said. "I've got a question for her."

She raised her eyebrows at me, and I nodded. Jordan, Hernandez, and I watched her walk off down the sidewalk until the building hid her from view.

"Pretty girl," Hernandez observed.

"Engaged to be married," I said.

"Hey. I'm just looking."

"So what's your question?" I asked Jordan.

He glanced around us. "Let's walk."

We did, Jordan on one side of me and Hernandez close on the other. Jordan said, "There's one thing that bothers me, something that seems out of character."

"What?"

His voice dropped almost to a murmur. "What made you think you could get away with throwing away a murder weapon? And if you were going to do it, why not a trash bin in an alley somewhere, preferably at night?"

I glanced at him. "Just for the sake of argument, let's say I did what the prosecutor accuses me of doing."

"Just for the sake of argument," Hernandez echoed on the other side of me.

I said, "I wouldn't have had access to the comparison bullet or a comparison microscope. I couldn't know it was the murder weapon."

"You could have a pretty strong suspicion," Jordan said.

"Yes, and if I guessed what I had was the murder weapon, I wouldn't want to toss it in an alley trashcan somewhere. It might never be found, and, as you say, it's a crucial piece of evidence."

"Evidence of your client's guilt."

"Evidence of how the crime was committed. I myself don't think Willow did it. Even if I did, I couldn't just dispose of the gun. It wouldn't be ethical."

"So why not turn it over to the police?"

"If I turn it over to the police, then Biggs knows it came from me, and he assumes it came from my client. A jury's likely to assume the same thing. If the gun didn't come from my client, if it was planted in my desk drawer by a person or persons unknown, that wouldn't be fair."

"It's exactly the spot you're in now."

"Yes, it is."

"Only worse," Hernandez said.

"Only worse. Good police work, bad luck…in any case, the frame someone dropped around Willow Woodruff and me has stuck."

"Speaking hypothetically," Hernandez said, opening the back door of their Explorer for me.

"Speaking hypothetically." I pushed in my briefcase and stepped in. Hernandez closed the door.

We were halfway across downtown when Jordan turned in the shotgun seat and said, "So what's the favor you wanted?"

I told him.

"That sounds like a pretty time-consuming proposition," Hernandez said.

"I said it was a favor."

"And you're the one who told her we were always at the disposal of the defense bar," Jordan told Hernandez.

"It was just a way of talking, for heaven's sake."

"Words have meaning," I said.

"Yeah," Hernandez said. "I've heard that somewhere."

They dropped me in front of my office. I took the stairs up, then, rather than go through the double doors, walked down the long hall so I could enter the executive suites through the back door. It required a key, but of course I had one. I came to Carter Fox's office before I got to mine, but his door was closed and no light shone under it. I stepped into the alcove to knock on his door, my subpoena at the ready.

There was no answer. Possibly, he had heard from Peyton what happened in court and was in hiding. When I got to the lobby, I asked Carly if she'd seen Carter Fox.

"No, not all day. He's been going to court to watch you."

"Not today. I wonder if you could manufacture some excuse to knock on his door and, assuming he doesn't answer it, open it and take a look inside."

She looked furtively around us. "You want another look?" she said.

"Not necessarily. You could just tell me what his office looks like, if it's been cleaned out or anything." Or if his body was sprawled across his desk.

She nodded, birdlike, and stood. "I'll be just a minute."

Brooke wasn't back yet—possibly she was still walking from the parking garage—and even Rodney's door was closed. I let myself into my office, unslung my briefcase and sat to wait for Carly. She was gone only a couple of minutes, but I was feeling the stirrings of unease when she came back.

"It all looks the same," she said from my doorway. She came in and said in a lower voice, "That envelope with the keys is still in his drawer."

I nodded.

"What's going on, can you tell me?"

"It's too early to say." We weren't in court, and what I said was no longer covered by privilege. Telling Carter's landlord that he was a crooked huckster and quite possibly a murdering psychopath would leave me open to a suit for defamation—unless of course it was all true. "I'll let you know as soon as I can." I smiled at her. "I know you like a good story."

"If there's something to know about someone, I like to get the goods," she said, holding up her hands and rubbing her thumbs and fingers together.

I had to laugh.

"See you, Robin. You stay safe."

She turned out of my doorway and was gone. My cell phone began to vibrate, barely audible down in my briefcase. I dug it out. It was Paul.

"Hey, Paul."

"Where are you?"

"My office, where are you?"

"Driving in from Roanoke. I'm almost there."

"It'll be good to have you back."

"You're not…you haven't been…"

"Arrested? You must have been talking to Brooke."

"She called me. She made it sound like a near thing."

"It's been postponed. We'll finish up the preliminary on Monday, and then they'll arrest me."

"That's not good."

I laughed. "Paul Soldano, master of the understatement," I said.

"Do you have a plan?"

"Sure. Find Carter Fox, serve him with a subpoena. Turn him inside out once I've got him on the stand. He might be too clever for me, but it's what I've got."

"Are you safe?"

"Safe?"

"The way Brooke tells it, Carter Fox may have already killed one person. I don't think he'd scruple at two."

"But he loves me. He gave me roses."

Paul didn't say anything.

"I'm kidding. I'll be careful. Did Brooke say where she was going? I thought she'd be here by now."

"She said something about getting a call from a client. I don't know."

"Glad you were paying attention. Can I assume that your fellow bank examiners are in the car with you, listening to your side of the conversation?"

There was a silence. "Maybe," he said.

"Who you got?"

He gave me three names, two of which I recognized. I heard two or three hey-Robin's in the background.

"Call me before you leave your office this afternoon," he said. "I'll come over and walk with you."

"I'm thinking of going home now," I said. "I need to decompress, spend an afternoon with my puppy."

"He's not a puppy. He's a sixty-five pound dog."

"And still growing. Just come over when you get off work. You can sit on the couch and watch me do aerobics."

"I'll bring take-out. What would you like?"

I told him to surprise me. When I'd hung up, I called Rodney Burns on his cell. "Where are you?" I asked him.

"I'm working." After a moment he continued, "I do get other jobs, you know. Fortunately for me."

"So what does this other client have you doing?"

"I hate to tell you."

I waited.

"I'm parked outside a bank on Midlothian Turnpike waiting to see who one of the loan officers takes to lunch. If he goes to lunch, that is. His wife seems to think…" He trailed off.

"That he's meeting someone for a nooner? Rodney Burns! You're off stirring up marital problems."

"I think of it as exposing marital problems that were there already. Did you need something?"

"Do you have a home address for Carter Fox?"

"No. Have you tried the internet?"

"I guess I will. You sound like you're going to be busy awhile."

"I could look it up for you on my phone."

"I'll do it." I hung up, but didn't reach for my computer mouse. I could do an internet search from home as well as from my office. The more pressing question was whether I wanted to eat lunch before I went home. I was hungry for food, but I was also hungry for home. I tucked my laptop and the subpoena for Carter Fox into my briefcase and headed out.

I got to my parking garage, but stopped on the sidewalk just outside the stairwell. I was looking for Carter Fox—suppose he was looking for me, too? An image came to me of him sitting on the steps in the dim light of the stairwell with a baseball bat resting on his shoulder. Carter was a small, flabby-looking man, but that didn't mean I wanted to meet him on the stairs.

I looked up and down 9th Street. At the corner, a man crossed on Cary Street, walking along the sidewalk. A couple of cars went by just beyond him, an SUV and a sedan. Back on Main was a steady flow of traffic. A light had turned. As nonthreatening as all that looked, it told me nothing about what was waiting for me on the stairs.

I bypassed the stairs, continuing down the hill to Cary Street and turning toward the automotive entrance to the garage. It was too warm a day to go slogging up and around one level after another, and by the time I got to my car, I was perspiring freely. I imagined Carter Fox sitting in the dim light of the garage's stairwell, hot and thirsty and increasingly hungry as he waited for me to show. I didn't really think he was there, but the image gave me a grim satisfaction.

I glanced at the door to the stairwell as I opened my car door and tucked my briefcase behind the driver's seat. I was being paranoid, I knew, but even paranoids have enemies. I didn't see any as I wound my way down out of the garage—no Carter Fox or Peyton Shilling, not even an Aubrey Biggs or Tom McClane—but that didn't mean they weren't all there, lurking just outside my field of vision.

At the exit onto Cary, I looked up the one-way street and pulled out into the flow of traffic. Aerosmith was on the radio, Steve Tyler singing about Janie and her gun, and I turned it up. If Robin was going to get a gun, maybe an M&P Bodyguard would be a good choice. On the other hand, it hadn't done Chris Woodruff much good, or Willow.

The radio station seemed to have fashioned a playlist from my favorites. By the time I got home, I was feeling mellow. I turned into the alley that ran behind my house. The garage door rumbled up, and I drove in. The door came down again behind me.

As I went in through the kitchen, I was humming and singing "Stairway to Heaven," though I was no singer, and it might have sounded more like I was strangling a chicken. I slung my briefcase with its laptop computer against the counter and carried my cellphone and my shoe-bag into the living room.

On the back side of the living room, one of the French doors was shattered and standing ajar. Not just the glass panes were shattered; the muntins that held them were cracked and broken as if a battering ram had burst the door inward. I took a step to put my back against a wall, my eyes darting. The door of my front closet was standing open, another indication that someone had been in my house. I had changed the locks, but it hadn't mattered. This time the intruder hadn't bothered with a purloined key.

After listening a moment and hearing nothing, I crossed to my front closet. Pushing the door further open, cringing at the faint creak, I crouched to reach for my brother's Louisville Slugger. It wasn't there. I pushed at the hanging jackets and the raincoat, moved around the basketballs and soccer ball and tennis balls, thinking a tennis racket, maybe even a racquetball racket, would make some kind of weapon, but no kind of bat or racket was there.

At a noise behind me, I turned my head. Carter Fox stood in the archway to the kitchen, cutting off my escape through the garage. I rose slowly, pushing the closet door shut behind me to open a path to the front door. Carter raised a hand.

There was a pistol in it, not one of the Woodruffs' Smith-and-Wesson Bodyguards—those were accounted for—but something like them. His index finger, I saw with unnatural clarity, was inside the trigger guard, and his knuckle was white with the pressure of his finger against the trigger.

"Unh unh unh," he said. The pistol was steady in his right hand, and his eye was visible just above the sight. It wasn't his only weapon. His left hand held a tire tool against his leg.

"Carter Fox," I said, but I croaked on the name and had to pause to work a bit of moisture into my suddenly dry mouth, expecting the blast of the gun at any instant. I tilted my head in the direction of the French doors. "Looks like you were anxious to get inside."

He smiled, his eyes unnaturally large behind his thick lenses. "Let's just say this time I want it to *look* like a break in. A home invasion by persons unknown." His white button-down was open at the collar, his dark chinos rumpled. Surgical gloves were on his hands.

"You weren't in court," I said, the hair at the nape of my neck stiffening and goosebumps breaking out on my arms.

"You never know how things are going to go in court, do you? Let's just say I didn't want to be present when sister-dear was on the stand."

"Peyton called you afterward, I take it."

"She called me. I'm afraid she said some things about you that weren't very nice."

"It is hard to imagine us ever being close friends," I said. I was still wearing the cotton dress I had worn to court, but also the running shoes I had put on for my walk to the parking garage. My briefcase was in the kitchen, my shoe-bag on the floor by my left foot where I had put it when I knelt to root through the closet. All I had for a weapon was the cellphone I held in my right hand.

Carter laughed, his customary series of nerdy honks, and, as his pistol came down slightly, the wavering end of the barrel pointed a foot or two above my head. I started to move, but Carter's hand steadied at once, and I froze.

"Always calculating the odds," he said. "That's one of the things I admire about you, Robin. So cool under pressure."

My pulse was beating palpably in my neck and in the palms of my hands. I was glad it didn't show. I said, "You brought me into this case, mailing me the murder weapon, making it appear and disappear. Why?"

"I've been following your career for a couple of years now. You're an exciting woman. I thought it would be a real turn-on to go up against you."

I felt my lip curl. "And was it? Was it good for you?" Movement through my front window caught my eye, but I resisted the impulse to turn my head. Across the street Dr. McDermott knelt by the bushes along the front of his house, possibly pulling weeds, his figure small and distant. He owned a pistol, I thought, but it would be inside the house. He wouldn't expect me to be home in the middle of the day, much less to be in trouble.

"What I really wanted," Carter said, "was to be on the inside, to get a blow-by-blow account of your development of the case. You don't seem to be especially close-mouthed. I get the idea your friends stay up-to-date on everything, professional confidences be damned, but I never made it to the inner circle." He shook his head. "Too bad. In the end you proved smarter than I thought—and I thought you were pretty smart to start with. I never expected you to tumble to what was going on with South of Main."

"So it was you who killed Chris Woodruff, not your sister Peyton."

"Doesn't make much difference at this point, does it?"

"Why not? You planning to shoot me?" The lamp on the nearby end table would be too clumsy a weapon, and I'd be dead before I could take the two steps to reach it.

"Maybe. It would be more fun to beat you to death, I think. And ballistics evidence is such a hassle." He raised the tire tool, keeping his pistol trained on my sternum. "Don't take it personally, Robin. In the game of life, sometimes you get beat." He gave a single honk of laughter. "Unless, of course, you cheat." He started toward me.

With a sharp, underhand motion I threw my cell phone at his face, and the gun went off as he flinched, the sound deafening. As the phone glanced off the top of his head, he swung the tire tool, but I stepped into him so that it was his hand rather than the tire tool itself that hit the side of my head. My arms closed around his body as I staggered, and I twisted to throw him away from me. The pistol went off in a second explosion, and Carter was on the floor, sliding, the pistol still in his hand and the barrel swinging toward me for a third shot. I took two running steps toward the front window and launched myself at it as the blast sounded.

The large pane of glass split silently amid the crash of the gun and its aftermath, but I felt it give and closed my eyes against the expected spray of glass splinters as I burst onto the lawn. I don't know what kind of glass the stunt actors jump through in the movies, but it probably isn't a double-paned picture window. I hit the glass, my forward progress halted, and I seemed to hang there as the pistol crashed again. A few big shards of glass fell outward while others remained like a double row of jagged teeth in the frame of the window. My body dropped onto the sill and sash with its up-thrust blades of glass, then spilled out onto spiked branches of the bushes that lined the front of the house. Pain blossomed like sheet lightening as Carter Fox loomed in the window above me. I rolled away from him, spilling onto the lawn, and Carter put a foot on the sill to leap after me, but his feet failed to clear the bushes completely so that he pitched forward and his hands and one knee came down on my hip and chest.

Numbness. Numbness and an unnatural clarity. I don't feel the impact—even that first stab of pain is gone as if it never was—but the numbness fails to alarm me. I have the sensation of rising, of looking down at my sprawled body, though my view is blocked by the little man with the oily black hair who is getting to his feet. The action is soundless. As my perspective grows, I see a brown animal streaking into the yard, its head and tail down as it devotes all its efforts to speed. Beyond the dog a white-haired man steps into the street, crossing toward my yard. In the silence the little man towers over my body, one arm rising with something in his hand, and the dog leaps into the air, hitting the man in the chest and throwing him backward into the bushes as the dog's jaws close on his face and its head jerks sideways, back and forth, as its jaws open and close again, and again.

An SUV lurches to a stop at the curb, and two men jump from it, one circling the car from the street side, both running, the first reaching the carnage at about the same time as the old man. The dog releases its hold on the black-haired man and spins, backing so that it stands between the men and my body, the fur on its back standing in a ridge. The old man stretches a hand toward the dog, palm out.

For a moment nothing seems to happen, then the dog lifts its head and moves toward the old man, tail wagging tentatively. One of the other men kicks at something with his foot and bends over the man on the ground. The third man has a hand to the side of his head, elbow out, and is gesticulating with his free hand.

The old man and the dog lean over me, are joined by one of the other men. The old man pushes at the dog with his elbow, and both men are laying hands on me, the old man directing with movements of his head. The third man drops his phone to the ground and tears open his shirt, a button flying as he yanks it off, and he throws the shirt at the old man, who snatches it out of the air and turns to slip it under and around my leg. I seem to be lying in a black puddle that is spreading even as it fades into the grass.

Another car stops in the street, and a man leaps from it and runs onto the lawn. I know him. He drops to his knees beside my body, and I try to say his name—Paul—but my lips don't move, and my eyes stare glassily upward.

Chapter 14

I wasn't dead, or, if I was, I didn't stay dead. I remember moments in an ambulance, and in those flashes of memory I am on my back, looking upward, and Paul is there, and a woman I don't know. The woman has her hair in a ponytail and is wearing a light blue shirt with a patch on the sleeve. I can't move my limbs, and something is strapped to my face.

There is a moment of bright lights and people in surgical masks around me.

Finally there is darkness and a peace free of pain and worry. I am not alone in the darkness. Someone is with me, a presence as big as a house and gentle as a mother, as I drift on a current of dreamless sleep.

When I came hard awake, it was only for an instant. I was in bed and the room was dimly lit and Paul Soldano sat slumped in a chair beside me. When I woke again, I was thirsty, and Dr. McDermott stood above me, looking down.

"Hey," I whispered.

"Hey. How do you feel?"

"Thirsty."

He stepped away from the bed. When he came back, he had a cup, and he spooned a little shaved ice onto my tongue. I nodded my thanks.

"You damaged your femoral artery coming through the window, and you lost a lot of blood," Dr. McDermott said. "Your blood pressure dropped, your body temperature dropped…" He took a breath and let it out. "I thought we'd lost you."

I moved my head in a slight nod.

"There was evidently some tricky repair work down there. You were in surgery nearly four hours, and it was three before a nurse came out with a positive prognosis."

"Carter missed me?"

"Carter…" Dr. McDermott's face cleared. "Oh. No, I forgot to mention that. There was also a bullet in your shoulder, but there wasn't much to it. It was lying up against the humerus, and they just took it out. The bullet, not the humerus." He touched my arm, and, twisting my neck, I saw the bandage.

"How much…blood…" I trailed off.

"How much blood did they give you? No whole blood, though you had a number of volunteers. You'd lost too much for that. They gave you packed red blood cells and fresh frozen plasma." After a moment he added, "Detective Hernandez has your blood type, if you want to tuck that away for future reference. You're both A-positive."

I closed my eyes, and I must have slept.

The next time I opened them, Brooke rose up next to me. "Paul, I think she's awake."

Paul appeared beside her. I looked up at them, and they looked down, neither speaking.

"Who died?" I said.

Brooke gave a little laugh. "Dr. McDermott said you'd been awake, but we weren't sure we believed him. Your mother, father, and brother are all here, but they're down in the cafeteria right now."

Paul said, "Those two cop friends of yours are out in the hall. They've been stopping by."

"Carter Fox. Is he..."

"Who cares," Paul said flatly.

Brooke laid a hand on his arm. "He wasn't as badly hurt as you," she told me.

"Though he looked a lot worse," Paul said. "I haven't seen him since he got his face and neck stitched up, but I imagine he's going to look like Frankenstein's monster."

"Your own face wasn't even scratched," added Brooke. "You do have some stitches in your right arm."

"And both legs, most of them in your left," Paul said. Brooke jabbed him with her elbow.

"Anyway," he said. "Deacon saved your life. I owe him a steak."

Brooke motioned with her hand, then went out into the hall. Paul stayed where he was as Hernandez and Jordan came in.

"You look better," Jordan said. "No thanks to us, I'm afraid. We were listening to everything, of course—"

"Even your singing," Hernandez said, "though it was a bit much."

"But we'd stopped for a couple bottles of water and were five minutes away when we realized you had a home invader."

"I think you've ruined 'Stairway to Heaven' for me forever."

The favor I had asked was for them to put a wire on me and record my conversations until I found Carter Fox. The world had changed since I'd seen cops taping a wire to Leonardo DiCaprio's belly, though. I'd just had to download an app onto my iPhone—something called Report-It, developed for news reporters, designed to broadcast high quality audio to a mobile receiver called a Phantom.

"But you got it," I said. "You've got a recording of everything he said."

"We've got it," Jordan said. "Already played it for Aubrey. He was a little slow to accept what he was hearing, but he did."

"You fighting for your life in the O.R. gave it a lot of credibility," Hernandez said.

My injuries must have given me credibility. The next day I was sitting up, waiting to be moved out of ICU into a regular room, when Aubrey Biggs himself came by just as visiting hours began. It was Saturday, and he was wearing jeans and sneakers. Since he was the height of a middle-schooler, the casual clothing made him look more like a boy than a grown man, much less the district attorney for the city of Richmond..

"You look like you're going to live," he said.

"Not quite the same as saying I'm looking good. I know. It'll be a relief to get my hair washed."

"I wasn't sure I should visit while you were still in ICU. I know we're often antagonists, and I don't want to elevate your blood pressure while you're recuperating."

"It's all right. Until this morning they were worried about my blood pressure being too low." I glanced at the monitors, but they'd been disconnected in anticipation of my move.

"I wanted you to know that the charges against Willow Woodruff have been dismissed, and she's been released. We've got a police officer posted at Carter Fox's door to take him into custody when the hospital releases him."

"Thank you for coming by to tell me. It's good to know things are wrapping up."

"Wrapped up, really. I'm not even going to file charges for the shell game you played with the guns." His quick smile looked more like a grimace of pain, though.

"One less battle to fight. Thank you."

"You really can't do things like that, you know."

I nodded. "One advantage to the police finding the gun in a neutral place, though, is that you couldn't place it in Willow's possession—and it didn't belong there. She never had it."

"It was her gun."

"From the murder on, she never had it," I amended.

"It was the murder weapon. You can't just throw it away." He was getting agitated, and I felt my own pulse quickening.

"Nobody threw it away," I said. "The police got an anonymous call almost immediately."

He gave me a long, speculative look. "The officer who took the call said the call came from a man."

I shrugged, and he sighed, shaking his head.

"You're going to make me old before my time, Starling."

The stream of visitors who came to see me in ICU had been pretty tiring, and I'd fallen asleep on them more than once. The group waiting for me in my new hospital room was a crowd—my mom and dad, Mike and Brooke, Willow Woodruff and Caden, and of course Paul. Even so, my brother wasn't there: he'd had to return to his medical practice in Charlottesville.

There was a cake, a big chocolate cake in the shape of a labrador retriever's head. "It was as close as we could come to bringing Deacon in to see you," my mother said.

"They have some kind of rule about letting deadly attack dogs roam the hospital corridors," Mike said.

"Deeks isn't deadly," I said.

"You should have seen Carter Fox when Deacon got through with him," Paul said.

"They're not…Nobody's talking about putting him down, are they?"

"Virginia does still have the death penalty," Mike said. "If you're talking about Carter Fox."

"I'm not talking about Carter Fox. I'm talking about…"

Paul took my hand. "We know. No. Nobody's talking about putting Deacon down."

"Defending another from imminent bodily harm is legal justification for the use of force," Mike said. "Evidently even for canines."

A tension went out of me that I hadn't known I'd been feeling.

Later in the afternoon, it was just Brooke and me. "I'm beginning to go stir-crazy," I said. "I need to get out of here. And Paul owes Deacon and me a steak dinner."

"I just heard him promise Deacon the steak dinner."

"We go together."

"You and Paul?"

"Me and…" I looked at her. "You know what I meant."

She nodded. "Mike and I are talking about a June wedding."

"You are. Wow! That's news."

"June 30 is a Saturday. What do you think?"

I moved my hand to the bed's controls and pushed the button to raise myself. "I think that's great," I said. "You know I'll be there. I'll be there with bells on."

"Have you ever been to a double wedding? It seems like it could be nice."

"A double wedding! Who else is getting married?"

"We thought maybe you and Paul."

"Who thought? You and Mike? You and Mike thought me and Paul?" I gave a laugh that came out sounding a little shaky. "You're premature on that one. He hasn't even asked me."

She nodded. "Maybe he hasn't had much encouragement."

I thought about it. "Maybe not," I conceded.

"He doesn't want to mess things up between the two of you."

"Life is full of risks," I said. "Faint heart never won fair maiden."

"Shakespeare?"

"I'm not sure, actually. Not Shakespeare, though."

"When do you get out of here? Do you know yet?"

"Soon, I hope. I'm going to press the doctor on it the next time I see him."

"When is that?"

I sighed. "Tomorrow morning, I'm afraid."

She left shortly after that. She, after all, had a life. I took a nap and dreamed a rather incoherent dream in which I was home with Deacon, and Paul was there, and I felt the same sort of peace I'd felt under the influence of anesthetic. When I opened my eyes, Paul was beside my hospital bed.

"You look miserable," I said, reaching for his hand. It was too far away, and I let my hand drop back onto the blankets. "Are you okay?"

He moved his head equivocally.

"Paul?"

"I've got something to ask you."

A fist of tension knotted my insides somewhere in the vicinity of my solar plexus. He opened his mouth, hesitated, closed it again without saying anything. I opened my own mouth, then closed it without saying anything either. Wordlessly, Paul placed a small, velour-covered box on the bedclothes over my abdomen.

I tucked my chin to look at it.

"It's a ring," he said, and my eyes cut toward him.

"I figured it was a ring," I said. A few seconds went by, but it felt like an hour.

"Do you want to see it?" he said.

I nodded. He reached for the box with both hands and opened it, his forearms resting against my side.

The ring was a thin gold band set with a marquis diamond that was bigger than it should have been.

"You can't afford this," I said.

"I've been saving."

My gaze went from the ring to his face. "If you ever cheat on me, I'll castrate you with the pruning shears. You know that."

A smile spread across his face like a ray of sunlight. "That sounds like a yes," he said.

I cut my eyes away from him. It did sound like a yes, didn't it? I met his eyes again and gave him a tentative smile.

"I guess it does," I said.

ABOUT THE AUTHOR

Michael Monhollon took out a semester in college to write science fiction stories and collect rejection slips. His first book sale, a legal thriller, came at the age of 31 at about the time *The Firm* was coming out in paperback. Its sales fell short of *The Firm*'s, though, and he continues to work for a living. For a dozen years he practiced law. Currently, he is a professor of business law at a small liberal arts college in Abilene, Texas.